I0632378

Frances Elizabeth Willard, Eliza Jane Trimble Thompson, Marie
Thompson Rives, Mary McArthur T. Tuttle

Hillsboro Crusade Sketches and Family Records

Frances Elizabeth Willard, Eliza Jane Trimble Thompson, Marie Thompson Rives, Mary McArthur T. Tuttle

Hillsboro Crusade Sketches and Family Records

ISBN/EAN: 9783337096663

Printed in Europe, USA, Canada, Australia, Japan

Cover: Foto ©Andreas Hilbeck / pixelio.de

More available books at **www.hansebooks.com**

HILLSBORO CRUSADE SKETCHES

AND

FAMILY RECORDS.

BY

MRS. ELIZA JANE TRIMBLE THOMPSON,
HER TWO DAUGHTERS,
AND
FRANCES E. WILLARD.

"Keep thy purpose with courage, and preserve an upright intention toward God."—THOMAS À KEMPIS.

CINCINNATI: CRANSTON & CURTS.
1896.

TO THE

WHITE-RIBBON WORKERS IN ALL LANDS,

𝕮HIS 𝖁OLUME

IS AFFECTIONATELY DEDICATED.

ELIZA JANE TRIMBLE THOMPSON.

HILLSBORO, OHIO,
    December 23, 1895.

THIS little volume is rightly introduced by some early family history, which, in its beginnings, "took methods and formed habits of truth" which outlasted many vicissitudes, and still serves as a legacy to children, grandchildren, and great-grandchildren.

M. McA. T.

CONTENTS.

7

ILLUSTRATIONS.

I.

THE MAKING OF AN EARLY GOVERNOR.

I.

THE MAKING OF AN EARLY GOVERNOR.

" The strenuous soul hates cheap success."—EMERSON.

NARRATIVES which begin with tomahawks and scalping-knives are not so sure of arresting attention in this advanced period of our American civilization as narratives which have to do with electricity and its effect upon poor criminals, or accounts of the advancements in marine architecture and how the " man-of-war " can best be built to withstand belligerents. But the tomahawk and scalping-knife were familiar sights to the pioneers of the seventeenth century, and, consequently, to the grandfather of our present chapter; and, finally, after many times witnessing the terrors of early warfare with these deadly weapons, he was himself attacked and killed by the Indians in the mountains of Virginia in 17ƒ3, shortly after he and his family emigrated to America: so that a tomahawk thrown across our pathway at this period of our story is significant.

John Trimble belonged to the Scotch-Irish race, and was a believer in John Knox, the man born at Giffordgate, a suburb of Haddington, in

1505, and who, before his death in Edinburgh,
1572, knew what intense hardships meant, as
well as remarkable experiences in affairs of
Church and State. As a believer in Knox and
his uncompromising doctrines and wonderful
zeal (which, an English ambassador said, "put
more life into Knox than six hundred trum-
pets"), our Scotch-Irish emigrant met his death
as heroically as John Knox would have met any
perpetrator of the massacre of St. Bartholomew.
"At the time that John Trimble was slain, James
his son, and his daughter Mrs. Estell, and a
black boy, were taken prisoners. Mrs. Estell was
sitting on a log, sewing ruffles on a shirt of her
husband, when the Indians claimed her as their
prize." "This marauding party was successfully
pursued over the Alleghany Mountains by a
party under Colonel Moffit, stepson of John
Trimble, who surprised and routed the Indians
and rescued the prisoners. James lived to aid
in punishing, in honorable battle, the slayer of
his father." "In 1774 he participated in the
bloody and decisive battle of Point Pleasant."*

"At the very beginning of the Revolutionary
War these savage tribes again took the field, and
the frontier settlements became the theater of

---

* Memoir of Mrs. Jane Trimble, by Rev. Dr. J. M.
Trimble. Published in Cincinnati, 1861. Methodist Book
Concern.

conflict between combined British and Indian forces and border troops. James Trimble commanded a company of these border troops during the war. In 1784 he decided to make the Territory of Kentucky his future home, and accordingly organized an emigrant company, which grew in such proportions that it finally numbered over five hundred souls. By the time it reached Bean's Station, a military commander, General Knox, of Revolutionary fame, was selected as leader. After traversing two hundred and fifty miles of wilderness, they reached Crab Orchard, Kentucky, November, 1784, and began to locate lands earned by military service." *

A late writer, who has been over this old wilderness road, says: "It has every conceivable badness—loose stone, ledges of rock, bowlders, sloughs, holes, mud, sand, deep fords, and one day in a wagon is enough to satisfy a man for life."

Our hero, the subject of this chapter, "the little governor," as he was afterwards called, was only twelve months old at the time referred to. It is impossible to see him, as he is wrapped in homespun blankets, clasped in his mother's arms, who is on horseback in the current of an angry river, the bravest woman in a party of five hundred emigrants! She clasps her baby very firm with one hand, and holds on with

* See Memoirs.

the other hand to the mane of her noble horse, and tells her other child to hold fast to her waist, and then plunges forward, arriving safely on the opposite shore, amidst the shouts of those who crossed before the river became so dangerous. General Knox shouted to her that, "after this, she should be his aid-de-camp and lead the women, as her husband, 'Captain James,' led the men." She made no reply, but knelt before the great army of people and offered a prayer of thanks to God for the narrow escape from death, amid their shouts and weeping.

When they reached Cumberland Gap, the old mountains looked dismal enough. "Twenty men were stationed by General Knox on the table-rock overhanging the 'Gap,' and twenty men were sent two hundred feet in advance of the main body of emigrants, which, as we have said, in all numbered five hundred souls. Two hundred of these were from Virginia, and the remaining number from North and South Carolina. The rocky and uncultivated approach to the 'Gap' was covered, in some places, by cane, growing ten feet high and as thick as hemp." But most of the party feared the panthers and wolves more than the canebrakes. Yet the canebrakes are said to be very difficult to penetrate, and in the extreme Southern States they grow to fifteen feet in height. "On the dividing line of Kentucky and Virginia they first began to appear. They were indicative of rich land, and in many instances usurp the growth of timber. The deer and the bear were fond of the young, green leaves, and as apt to hide in one of these canebrakes as were the Indians."

General Knox sent out a reconnoitering party, which was attacked by wolves and panthers, and barely escaped the stealthy Indians. They were now fast arriving at the frontier post. Buffaloes, bears, and deer furnished food for the people all winter.*

They settled on a farm in Woodford County, Kentucky, near Lexington—the famous Bluegrass Region—and there remained until they removed to Ohio in 1804. Captain James Trimble and his wife determined, after having lived in Kentucky for some time, to release their slaves. The captain presented his deed of manumission to the courts. It was twice refused, as an evil influence, which would exert itself over the servants of others; and not until young Henry Clay, with an eloquent request, had urged it, did the courts accept the noble deed. From that time (1802) there arose a friendship between Mr. Clay and the Trimble family, which continued during his life; and the correspondence between Henry Clay and Allen Trimble,

* Memoirs of Jane Allen Trimble.

2

who was, of course, younger, contained much
that is valuable in the political and social events
of those years.

Captain Trimble, after having liberated his
slaves, made arrangements to go to a free State
in 1804. "He took with him some help, purchased lands in Ohio, cleared ten acres, put
up a double log-cabin, planted a young orchard,
and returned to Kentucky to prepare his family
for the journey;" but, alas! was overtaken by
sickness and died, leaving his wife and eight
young children to find their own way to the free
State.*

The only time before this calamity that we
have seen our little hero was on the day when
he crossed the angry river, held tight in his
mother's arms, wrapped in his homespun blankets. Now he springs up, like a young Spartan,
and cheers the sad and weary heart of his
widowed mother, as she, with her "eight father-
less children, travels over the rough roads of this
unbroken country for six weary days, until she
reaches her home in the wilderness of Ohio."
The few improvements Captain Trimble had
been able to make rendered the spot dear to the
heart of his faithfu. widow, as it was his last
work on earth. A less brave, devout, and in-

* Facts related by Rev. J. M. Trimble in Memoirs referred to.

telligent woman than Jane Allen Trimble would have tarried in the former circle with older associations; but the very face of the woman shows what firmness as well as tenderness centered in her nature.

The widowed mother and her eight children prospered. Their home was a resort for many interesting and intelligent pioneers, and even Indians, with their squaws and papooses, would come in and stay for a meal, stand their papooses up against the wall in their cases while shaking hands in good faith with the woman whom General Knox had called his "aid-de-camp."

Two of the sons were sent to Philadelphia for their education. One became a physician, the other a merchant and a writer of history; another son, whose portrait shows a noble countenance, served in the War of 1812 as colonel, and afterward was a United States senator; and a younger son was sent to a classical school in an adjoining State. Three sons were engaged in military service. Carey was appointed to a lieutenantcy in the regular army. The sisters married Virginians, Mr. John Nelson and Mr. James McCue. Mrs. Trimble was greatly aided in the management of the family by her son Allen, who afterward, as governor of Ohio, just twenty-one years after the arrival of the family at the log-cabin, distinguished himself in his official duties. He served

the State in various capacities for twenty-five con-
secutive years. "Educational interests and in-
ternal improvements of every kind were encouraged and aided by him. Underlying all his success
in life, and the very source of his power, was integrity. He put a high estimate upon personal
honor, and bequeathed his descendants a spotless
name in public and private life."* He was very
fond of showing to his grandsons an old silver
soup-ladle, which had been made from some silver
won the first and only time he ever played cards
when a young man. He had it made, he said,
"to remind him of his folly and of his vow
never to play cards again for gain as long as he
lived." He was equally self-denying on the
temperance question, and while other men of his
generation kept their wines and brandy on their
sideboards, he never did, but made it a point,
even when hurried in his executive office, to
attend temperance conventions, and once took
his daughter "Eliza" to Saratoga to the first
National Convention. This was after the time
when, as a child of nine years, while attending
a private school in Cincinnati, the desperate
effort was made to kidnap the only daughter of
the governor. At this time little Eliza was at
Mr. Picket's school, in Cincinnati—a private
school for girls, and she boarded with Mrs.

---

* Biographical Sketch, by Rev. John F. Marlay.

McKnight, on Fifth Street, between Sycamore and Main, where sixteen other girls boarded.

It was the second term of Governor Trimble's administration. A case very rare in those days of a man killing his wife and two children occurred. The indignation was great; yet some hearts were sympathetic, believing the man to be not in his right mind. Although the law pronounced judgment of hanging, Mr. Alibone Jones, Dr. Daniel Drake, and others, got up a petition for the commutation of his sentence to lifetime imprisonment, setting forth the condition of the poor man. Governor Trimble, being very much inclined on mercy's side, accepted the proposition, and the sentence was commuted, and changed to life-time imprisonment. This caused much commotion and indignation among the rabble. Governor Trimble, Mr. Alibone Jones, and Dr. Drake were hung in effigy, and then burned, in the streets of Cincinnati. George Lair, who had been for years in service in the governor's family, was at the present time a stage-driver between Hillsboro and Cincinnati. He was devoted to the children of his former employer. One of his favorite horses being disabled, he left his hotel and went to the stable to take care of it. As he watched by the side of his horse he heard a whispering from men on the other side of the stall, who

were making a plot to carry the little daughter
of the governor off, conceal her in New Orleans,
and keep her as a hostage until the governor
would consent to have Burtsell hung. George
discovered that they knew her boarding-place.
He determined to go at daybreak to Judge John
McLean's home, who was one of Governor Trimble's intimate friends. Finding from the butler,
who met him at the door, that Judge McLean
was in Washington, he went immediately to the
house of Mr. George Jones, the father of Mr.
Alibone Jones; for his wife, Mrs. Jones, and
daughter had visited Hillsboro when George was
coachman for Mr. Trimble. When Mrs. Jones
became aware of the situation, she told George
she would call at an early hour for Eliza, at the
boarding-house, and take the little one for a
drive. She assured Mrs. McKnight she had
permission from her parents for a visit from
the little girl, and would keep her several
days.

When she had the child safely at home with
her, she told her frankly the situation, and
warned her not to leave the house, unless pro-
tected by her husband or son. Mrs. Jones was
much fortified to find great bravery on the part
of the child. She wrote to Governor Trimble,
that " Eliza was neither agitated nor frightened."
She took her to the school in her carriage, and

acquainted Mr. Picket with the facts. Eliza sat quietly there, making quill pens with her old teacher, while Mrs. Jones went farther on her rounds that morning. When she called for Eliza, she found her as composed as any little philosopher.

Mr. Trimble wrote that, as soon as he could, he would devise a plan to get her home safely, but that he was advised by Dr. Drake and Mr. Jones not to venture into the city himself. Eliza remained with Mrs. Jones for two weeks, and then she was taken care of by Mrs. Judge McLean for three weeks, at the end of which time her little brother Cary and George Lair came in the stage-coach to take her home. They had to feign their names, and did not talk to each other on the journey. One day and a night were required for the journey from Cincinnati to Hillsboro in those days, which now is made in three hours. The stage stopped in Williamsburg, and the little girl was put into a bed in a room next to the bar, where the men all night cursed her father.

As a matter of history, it is interesting to recall that Mrs. George (Bank) Jones, as she was called, because her husband was a banker, was a Miss Alibone, of Philadelphia, and once, on her way from that city to Cincinnati, she took the route through Hillsboro. She carried gold and silver coin in her carriage to her husband's bank, and feared to stay at the hotel, so Mr. and Mrs. Trimble invited her to remain at their house, little supposing that she would return the kindness in the manner just related.

The first wife of Allen Trimble was Margaret McDowell, a clever woman, of great animation of manner and good heart. They were married in 1806, in Woodford County, Kentucky. She was the sister-in-law of Mrs. General McDowell, who took so active a part in the Ohio Crusade. "Her father was Major Joe McDowell, a statesman and soldier in North Carolina of distinction, one of the leaders of the North Carolina troops at King's Mountain—the fatal battle of the Revolution in the South. The great victory won there over the British arms drove Cornwallis into Virginia, where he was compelled to surrender to Washington, and the success of the Colonies' cause was assured. McDowell was then elected to the Convention which formed the constitution of North Carolina. For years he represented his people in the North Carolina Legislature and Senate, and, after many years of service in the National Congress, he moved to Kentucky, where his life closed, and where he left many debtors to his usefulness and high reputation in the future generations which still honor his memory."

Allen Trimble served in the War of 1812, under Harrison, and was commissioned major. William and Cyrus, his brothers, were also in this war; Colonel William A. Trimble being desperately wounded in the sortie at Fort Erie under General Brown, which caused him to resign his position in the army, and in 1817 he was elected to the United States Senate by the Legislature of Ohio. He died in Washington City in 1821, at the age of thirty-five, where the writer of this chapter recently visited his grave in the Senatorial Cemetery.

Allen Trimble took his seat in the first General Assembly that ever convened in the city of Columbus, Ohio, and was returned seven successive terms, and in 1818–19 he was chosen president of the Senate. Those who can judge, speak within the limits of truth and justice when they affirm he was the ablest presiding officer the Senate of Ohio has ever had.*

The loss of his first wife was grievously felt by him and by his two little boys, Joseph and Madison. In 1811 he became imbued with the spirit of a young and beautiful Quakeress, of auburn hair, mild blue eyes, and mild temperament, which, as Hamlet says, "doth give the torrent smoothness." Her parents, Mr. and Mrs. Woodrow, were elegant, dignified Quakers, and she was educated to

---

° Biographical Sketch, by Rev. John F. Marlay.

be a true woman. She was the mother of Cary
A. Trimble, William H. Trimble, and Eliza
Jane Trimble Thompson. There was in this
marriage, cemented by religious sentiment and
common interests in serious topics, a vast influence, extended through long and useful years,
until, as old people of eighty and seventy-seven,
they smiled in mutual sympathy upon each other
across their glowing fireside, and upon their children, grandchildren, and great-grandchildren,
urging lessons of integrity, industry, and patience
upon all who came in their way. Many a time
has the writer of this sketch sat midway between
these noble grandparents and read aloud the
volumes of Washington Irving's "Life of Washington," many instances of which were very
familiar to their ears; so much so that they
would interlace family legends and Revolutionary
stories with the historical facts given by the
author. A curious illustration of the patience
and sagacity of Allen Trimble and his wife
"Rachel" is the story of the two thousand dollars. One morning, in midwinter, they were
startled, while making their toilet, by the old
colored cook, "Patsey," giving a tremendous
knock at their door, and calling out: "Hurry
out here, Miss Rachel, for the Lord's sake!"
Accustomed to all manner of people and events
in those early days, Mr. Trimble opened the

door halfway and saw James Brooks, one of his Fayette County farm superintendents, trying to push his way in, and, while grasping the hand of his employer, he cried out, "I'm a ruined man, governor. Here's all that's left," and he threw down on the table a mangled, wet, and hideous-looking pocket-book.

"That's just the way it looked," said he. "Betsey can swear to it, when I took it out of the gluttonous beast's throttle! That's the way it looked, and that's all that's left of the two thousand dollars!" And he clenched his teeth and said: "I'm at your mercy, governor; will work it out if it kills me!"

"Lock the door behind us," said Mr. Trimble. "Come, James, and have your breakfast, and after that we'll talk it over. Come, Rachel," said he to his wife; "lock the door and bring the key."

After breakfast the fragments were taken from the pocket-book, which James explained was in the pocket of his blouse when he was feeding the gluttonous beast (and the rest of the critters, as he called them), who turned and snatched the pocket-book instead of the fodder, and began chewing up two thousand dollars of bank-notes as fast as if they'd been grass. "I took to my heels for the house," said he; "snatched my gun from the shelf, and Betsey startin' after me, thinkin' I was going to kill myself; but I made straight for the greedy ox, and I ripped open his throat in no time, and there it was! Sure enough, there it was! Nasty, villainous thing! But I'll work it out, governor; I'll work it out, if it kills me."

"Do n't get so excited, James," said Mr. Trimble. "We'll see what can be done;" and he took up the wet mass of paper and said to his wife: "Can you have the patience to spread these separate pieces out on a table, if some one helps you, until they dry, and then paste them on tissue paper, reconstructing the face of the bills if possible; the bank may yet receive them at some discount." Little Eliza was allowed to stand on a chair by the table, and watch her mother and one of her uncles all day, while they separated and combined this "filthy lucre." The banks received the notes, finally, making only a small discount. Poor James wanted to bear the loss; but the governor paid him a premium instead, for his brave and honorable conduct.

Mrs. Trimble and the family resided in Hillsboro during the years of Mr. Trimble's executive work in Columbus, and he always claimed that the repose and strength he received during the short vacations in his Hillsboro home replerished his mind for its labors and public cares:

believing that "the only heart that can help us
is one that draws, not from society, but from
itself, a counterpoise to society;" and he con-
trasted the quiet, beautiful, and industrious life
of his wife with the gay extravagance of other
women whom he constantly met, and felt as
much comfort and pride as a man can feel in
the knowledge that he has a perfect companion.
Mrs. Trimble's taste for all that was pure and
beautiful showed itself in her finely-selected,
half-Quaker toilets; her choice of good old ma-
hogany furniture and beautiful china; her culti-
vation of flowers; and her exquisite table—for
never was there a more perfect housekeeper.
Once while Miss Katherine Beecher was visiting
Mrs. Trimble she inquired of Miss Katherine
what subjects she was writing upon just then?
"Housekeeping," Miss Beecher answered, ami-
ably. "How would you enjoy some practical
experience in that line?" said Mrs. Trimble;
"I can furnish you with some to-day." "O!"
said Miss Beecher, "it is so much easier to
write about than to put into practice."

II.

HIS ONLY DAUGHTER.

II.

HIS ONLY DAUGHTER.

SUNDAYS were representative days in the old Hillsboro home, and the visits of children, grandchildren, and great-grandchildren made the grandparents' hearts glad, even after the infirmities of extreme old age prevented them from attending Church services. It had been their habit to drive to the Methodist Church (of which they were loyal members, the Presbyterian and Quaker belief having fused itself into the religion of the Wesleys) in their elegant, tasteful carriage. This carriage was a great source of pride to the grandchildren, who were not allowed to touch the dove-colored cloth and silk, nor even the ivory buttons, or disturb the composure of the white horse. They could enjoy the horses " Red-bird " and " Jenette " and " Pony," but not " grandma's white church-horse," as they call it.

Dr. Joseph M. Trimble, the oldest of Governor Trimble's sons, after an active and useful life in the ministry of the Methodist Church, located in Columbus, Ohio. He was well known throughout the State, and represented his Church

3

at the General Conferences for many years. He had a large interest, as his father had, in educational institutions, to one of which he left a handsome endowment. He was possessed with the spirit of reform, of self-sacrifice, of firm and abiding religious conviction. He married Sarah Starr, a niece of General Trimble, of Baltimore, who assisted him in a cheerful manner in all he undertook. She still lives to enjoy the abundance of good his industry and wisdom surrounded her with. Of her cheerful Christian virtues much could be written.

Mr. James Madison Trimble, the second son, married a daughter of Mr. John Smith, of Hillsboro, a wealthy citizen. Mrs. Trimble was a woman of just pride and dignity of character. Their large and interesting family added greatly to the pleasure of Governor and Mrs. Trimble's life, as they resided in Hillsboro in a handsome property near by. Mr. Madison Trimble resembled his father in appearance, and had the same sense of humor and keen wit and talent for accumulating money, and the same enjoyment of political affairs. These two oldest sons were children by the first marriage. Wm. H. Trimble, Cary A. Trimble, and Eliza Jane Trimble were the children of the second marriage. Dr. Cary A. Trimble, who was well known in the medical profession, married Mary McArthur, the youngest

daughter of Governor Duncan McArthur, of
Chillicothe, Ohio, a woman of rare beauty. His
second marriage was to Anne Porter Thompson,
a sister of Hon. James H. Thompson. Dr. Trimble represented his district most ably in Congress.
He was a man of the world, courteous and interesting. The double tie of relationship, brought
about by his marriage with Mr. Thompson's sister,
was most happy for both families, and their son
Allen, named for Governor Trimble, was a very
unusual boy, as was the daughter by the first
marriage with Mary McArthur. Mrs. Trimble's
rare intelligence, and exemplary taste in Washington life and in their Chillicothe, Columbus,
and Florida home, is still a matter of pride to all
her relations.

Colonel Wm. H. Trimble married Martha
Buckingham, of Zanesville, Ohio, the youngest
daughter of Ebenezer Buckingham, a man of
large wealth and high business qualifications
Colonel Trimble was full of energy, ambition,
and public spirit, and it was an hereditary in-
clination which led him into the War of the
Rebellion. His home was the result of fine
taste and costly selections made by his wife.
Landscape gardening was much studied by them
both, and good architecture. Their place called
"Woodland," a suburban residence, is now owned
by Mrs. Trimble's nephew, Rev. George Beecher,

nephew of Henry Ward Beecher. He has built
a costly gray-stone house also in this beautiful wooded lawn. The three children of Colonel and Mrs. Trimble, alas! died in the bloom
of youth and fortune, leaving beautiful characters.

Now we come to Eliza Jane Trimble, the only
daughter, who married James Henry Thompson,
September 21, 1837, when a girl of twenty-one.
It was a marriage blest with the approval of
parents and the extravagant enthusiasm of
friends. On the morning when the bridal party
started on the wedding journey the sun shone
out in all its splendor. The carriage occupied
by the bride and groom, groomsman and brides-
maid, had come from Kentucky with its colored
driver, an old family servant, who felt the vast
responsibility resting upon him to bring the
bridal party in safety back to Kentucky.

To Governor Trimble and his wife it was a
serious fact that their only daughter was now
married. This spirited girl of twenty-one, weigh-
ing only ninety pounds, with wavy, auburn-
brown hair (or "chestnut sorrel," as her husband
called it), brown eyes, and an unusually fine and
lofty forehead, had married a courteous, industrious, and talented young lawyer, whose family
was in perfect harmony with her own. He
was a man destined to claim, now and then,
in his long laborious life, the luxury of being a

dreamer. On his wedding-day he luxuriated in this way, and was consequently very silent. Finally, being questioned by his groomsman, who sat opposite to him, on his behavior, he exclaimed:

"Can't you let me spend one day in silence, thanking God that Eliza was ever born?"

"O yes," said Mr. Mathews, "excuse me for even giving you an incidental glance. Being myself an old bachelor, I did n't know what etiquette required toward a bride. I had always supposed the groom spoke to her occasionally;" whereupon the whole party roared out laughing, and the colored driver whipped the horses into a terrible speed.

Harrodsburg, Mercer County, Ky., was a home similar in history to the one in Ohio, which had given to the young, promising lawyer his wife. Much hospitality and much admiration was awaiting the young couple. Even the slaves were joyful over the appearance of so much festivity.

" Lord 'a' mercy," said old black mammy, "Mr. Henry never tire pettin' the young bit of a bride, little enough to put into his pocket."

The "generous hospitality, beautiful women, and fine horses," for which Kentucky is noted, were fully appreciated by the young Ohio bride. "Montrose," the home of the groom, was much more to the bride's taste than the elegant place

38522

of Colonel George Thompson, their uncle, so
celebrated, with its three thousand acres, three
hundred slaves, deer-park. Dinner-parties served
with silver-covered dishes, and extravagance in
all directions; and while she had presided at her
father's table, even when a child, over large
political dinners (during the ill-health of her
mother) on important occasions—for instance,
when De Witt Clinton, governor of the State of
New York and his staff were present—yet the
main thread of her life had been one of industry
and economy, except her Cincinnati education,
which was then considered a luxury, and her visits
to Boston and Saratoga with her father; and she
claimed little knowledge of the big world, but
instinctively she knew it; and it was this keen
insight into human nature and human affairs
which was to distinguish every action of her
life. As a child she had been made to rise at
midnight and pray with her grandmother (with
whom she slept); to rise at daybreak, and ride
on horseback with her father; and to sit by her
mother, and complete tasks which were the most
irksome sometimes to her little spirited nature.
Yet discipline was believed in by the parents.
She had been taught that to treat divine things
frivolously was wicked. And so the spirit of Kentucky society, with its wit and humor and gay-
ety, and its fields of sport, was novel to her

mind. After having enjoyed this peep into the Sunny South, so different in its conventionalities and social usages from the Middle and Northern States, the bride and groom returned to Ohio.

After residing with Governor Trimble in Hillsboro for a short time, they went to Cincinnati to live. The life there was among the most congenial friends, and Mr. Thompson's rank at the bar was high, as his colleagues were always willing to admit.

Little "Allen" and "Anna," the first children, were tenderly and daintily cared for. The fine old gardens of Nicholas Longworth were in the near neighborhood, and afforded a charming resort for the children, as the social life at this unusual home did for the parents. Many years afterward, Mrs. Thompson took her two younger daughters, Marie and Mary,* by invitation, to visit at this old mansion, where the millionaire of Cincinnati, in his old age, walked about among the various members of his household, like a little king out of some fairy story.

Mr. Thompson, although a Kentuckian by birth, came of Virginia parents, John B. Thompson and Nancy P. (Robards) Thompson. He was the third child in a family of ten children.

---

* These children wanted the same name, and were gratified when their parents told them one might be French and the other English Mary.

His grandfathers were both officers in the Revolutionary army, one a colonel, and one a captain. His father was a lawyer, who achieved an enviable reputation at the bar and in local statesmanship. He was of English and Scotch blood, and his mother was of Welsh and French Huguenot blood. Mr. Thompson's brothers, Hon. John B. Thompson, United States senator from Kentucky, and Philip B. Thompson, one of the leading spirits of the Kentucky bar, and his brother Charles Thompson, were men like himself—possessed of energy and ability. His five sisters were superior women. One of them married the youngest brother of his wife, Hon. Cary A. Trimble. So these Virginia families, the Thompsons and the Trimbles, were by ties related by blood, by profession, and by sympathy.

From 1838 to 1842 Mr. and Mrs. Thompson remained in Cincinnati, but removed to Hillsboro on account of its more healthful climate, where they have ever since resided. Mr. Thompson always engaged in a large circuit practice of five surrounding counties, also in the circuit and district courts of the United States, of Ohio, and in the Supreme Court of the State. (Biographical History of the Scioto Valley, page 203.) "In the reports of this court his name and arguments appear as counsel from 1840 to 1894, as many times, if not more, as are the number of the vol-

umes of the Reports; but his best reputation was achieved as a land lawyer, in the complex titles of the Virginia Military District."

"At the time they removed to Hillsboro, Governor Trimble and Mr. Thompson were both ardently supporting General Harrison, the old-line Whig, and in 1844 he took an active and prominent part in favor of Mr. Clay, and at the last Whig Convention at Baltimore urged the nomination of General Scott. At the beginning of the War of the Rebellion he threw his influence with the Republican party. "His family were residing in the beautiful home which he had planned and built, a place which to-day is called "Forest Lawn." My first recollections of my mother come from these days, which afforded me a joyful childhood. The face, the form, the walk, and the voice left an impression upon me as a child, of a spiritual nature, of a being from whom much light in the home radiated. But little did I think of all that mother's face and form and walk and voice would be to me in after years. There was a charm about my father which captivated and fascinated me. The cheerful hospitality of Mr. and Mrs. Thompson in those days in their beautiful home was most generous.

A school-friend of Anna Porter Thompson has latetly written the following paragraphs: "Years went by; the spacious mansion and surrounding

groves echoed with the sound of children's tiny
feet, and were full of the music of baby voices.
Allen grew toward manhood a wonderfully beautiful boy—such as we dream Absalom may have
been—his hair of a flaxen tinge, his eyes blue as
the skies of old Highland, his voice vibrant with
a boyish melody, which never left it, even in his
mature years. He left the University of Delaware to enter the ministry, and married a handsome brunette girl, the daughter of Rev. Dr.
George Crum. The parent's hearts were filled
with pride and content as they realized how bril-
liant the young clergyman was, what a power in
the Church, what pathos and what eloquence;
but sorrow began to trace deep lines on the faces
of the joyful parents." "Anna, their oldest and
beautiful daughter, had developed at the age of
eighteen into a fine and noble womanhood,
"when the angels came," says her classmate,
"and laid white roses on her pulseless breast,
and shut out forever the light from her soul-
inspiring eyes." But the crushed mother said:
"Thy will be done." "It was the faith which
had fed the Trimble blood for generations,"
says this writer, "that compelled her to be still,
and know that it was God." A fortitude more
heroic, a resignation more exalted than the after
life of the poor, bereaved mother, is not for record;
but to Mr. Thompson there came no surcease of

grief, and learned though he was, says this same writer, "he found no balm in Gilead." "Thou wilt come no more, gentle Anna," he exclaimed, as he walked the spacious house over; but "the eternal womanhood led her husband on," and he united with the Church, and tried also to say, "Thy will be done." He had interested himself in helping to build the Hillsboro Female College, and now, although Anna, one of its first gradutes was gone, Marie and Mary were still to be educated.

The declining years of Governor and Mrs. Trimble claimed the attention of their only daughter. Mr. and Mrs. Thompson moved to the old residence with the children. Forest Lawn was sold to Mr. Joseph Richards, who still occupies and improves it each year, and the family henceforth resided, as they do to-day, under the old ancestral roof.

The sad days of the War of the Rebellion were closing in about all, and Joseph, the second son, entered the army, while Allen, the oldest son, was raising his eloquent voice before crowded audiences, in pulpits and lyceums over the great plan of salvation, and the war for freedom. He exclaims, on a Fourth of July, when making an oration:

"On this day, shame upon the man who would obtrude his political prejudice, or theolog-

ical dogma, or private pique, as an apple of dis-
cord upon the festive, joyous, heart-dancing as-
semblies of the free! Nay, this is the day to
prove the poet's inspiration and truthfulness,
who sang,

> 'Divide as we may in our own native land,
>   To the rest of the world we are one.' "

He had, in those days, charge of the large
Wesley Chapel of Cincinnati; but the enormous
duties it brought, the vast audiences, together
with domestic cares, were too much for him.
Discouragement and insufficiency began to take
hold of his strong nature. Must he be defeated
for want of endurance? Had he miscalculated
his strength, or would he not glory in the conflict of life. These were the thoughts brought
keenly before him every day. By "acting rashly
he might buy the power of talking wisely." (Emerson.)

His gentle-hearted wife, with her dark,
handsome eyes, looked on with admiration, believing that he would long live to assail the
powers of darkness, and plead for the elevation
of the masses. But a sad and silent elapse
of his work, of his energies, followed for a
short time, and then once more he came forth,
like one who had been captured by an enemy.

but suddenly released, and on the rostrum and in the pulpit, even of Henry Ward Beecher's, he held vast crowds entranced. There came another Fourth of July, when, after an oration, he took cold, and, pneumonia following, he struggled into the new birth of the life to come with the following words on his lips: Though suffering intensely, he was well aware, he said, "that the icy stillness of promised death had settled upon him." He called for his wife, had his little daughter Sallie on one side, and his son George on the other, and clasping them in silence, he offered his wife and children his last embrace. (See "Memoirs of Allen T. Thompson," published in 1868.)

In the memoirs many resolutions, such as the following are to be found:

"He loved the cause we still love to honor and perpetuate, and we deem it but a small return for what he has done and suffered, that we inscribe our tribute of respect and regard upon the tablets which commemorate his virtues, and never-to-be-forgotten labors among us. But he has passed to his reward, calmly and sweetly, as the true Christian sinks to rest, leaving us to mingle our tears, and offer our deepest sympathy and kindest regards to his bereaved and heart-stricken family."

He had begun writing his autobiography, and among other paragraphs this one, regarding his mother, appears:

" I can not refrain from a moment's tribute to her—my mother—whose hand of sympathy was never refused, and whose tremulous words of wise warning and kind entreaty, never ceased till its mournful cadence was changed for the subdued, but no sweeter tone of present praise; who seems to me now more like an angel, too pure for earth, but left awhile in Divine mercy to woo and win souls to Jesus and heaven."

This experience and death was a serious blow to the entire family. The old governor mourned for his namesake; but the martyr heart of Mrs. Thompson spoke in language bold, clear, and courteous to those who came to offer sympathy.

The widow and children came to the old home, and were tenderly cared for. These old rooms, with their large windows, the panes of glass so small and numerous, still let the light of heaven in. The wood-fires burned brightly, and the high, old mantel-shelfs, with their Doric columns painted black and faced with red brick, and the red hearths upon which stood elegant brass fire-irons supporting the big logs, all looked very quaint and attractive to the little ones. The glow of the fire fell upon some portraits on the opposite wall, and lighted up the

rich old family heirlooms; and "Grandma Thompson," as they called my mother, sat in her rocking-chair, with her foot on a footstool, while her fingers flew among the wool and steel needles to make little stockings for her grand-children, as she had made them for her darling boy Allen. There were now, during the war times, five generations, fourteen people at the table of Governor Trimble.

Marie and Mary visited in Cincinnati, and in 1870 Marie was married to Dr. Edward Rives, a gifted man of high family birth and unusual education. Mary went to Europe to study art. Herbert Tuttle, whom she met abroad—a man of rare character and attainments, who was then the Berlin correspondent of the London *Daily News* a native of Bennington, Vermont—came to Hillsboro, where they were married, July 6, 1875, at the old homestead. They lived in Europe for four years. On their return to America, Mr. Tuttle, as teacher and historian, distinguished himself among scholars. Dr. Rives and his wife left Cincinnati for the better climate of Hills-boro, where the doctor's large experience as lec-turer and practitioner in the medical profession was highly estimated. Mrs. Rives, since the death of her husband, has been a beautiful ex-ample of unselfish devotion to parents and joy to friends.

Joseph, the second son, at the close of the war went to the far West, where, after several years engrossed with the fascinations of that life and climate, he lost his life after heroic endurance. And it was thought that the anguish which my mother experienced over this the death of her third child would terminate her own life. But life is not terminated by grief, else would few survive the terrible stroke.

Henry, the third son, graduated in the medical college of Cincinnati, but declined to practice medicine, preferring the business life with his youngest brother, John Burton Thompson, in Colorado. They plunged into pioneer life, as their forefathers had done. The unselfishness of Henry and John Burton in financial affairs, and the generosity of the daughters, make the old age of Mr. and Mrs. Thompson serener than it could otherwise be.

Sallie, the daughter of Allen Thompson and Lucy, his wife, the beautiful blonde, married John A. Collins, of Hillsboro, son of Charles A. Collins, the lawyer and poet. After a few years of happy married life in Hillsboro, the young lawyer preferred to go West—to beautiful Puebla—where Sallie died, so young and so beloved.

George, the son, resides at Xenia, with his mother and his wife, Maude (daughter of Colonel

Thomas, of London, O.), and two little flaxen-haired babies, the great-grandsons of Judge and Mrs. Thompson, who are coming, as these lines are being written, to brighten the old ancestral home with the ring of their childlike glee.

4

III.

HILLSBORO CRUSADE SKETCHES.*

"And he said to them all, If any man will come after me, let him deny himself, and take up his cross daily, and follow me.

"For whosoever will save his life, shall lose it: but whosoever will lose his life for my sake, the same shall save it."—LUKE IX, 23, 24.

*From the *Union Signal*, Chicago, May 4, 1895.

Sketch

IT is an old saying, and true as it is old, that God not only raises up people for emergencies, but also fits them for these by special opportunities, and often by trials. The writer of these sketches, a daughter of Hon. Allen Trimble, one of Ohio's honored governors, was born in Hillsboro, Ohio, August 24, 1816. She grew up in a home characterized by comfort and culture, and careful training. To the educational advantages which an intelligent community afforded her, were added those of the schools of Cincinnati, as well as of acquaintance with many of the prominent people of the day.

Her marriage to the Hon. James H. Thompson, September 21, 1837, brought her union with one of intellectual tastes and of unusual mental gifts. The heart of her husband has proudly trusted in her, and most lovingly have her sons and daughters risen up to call her blessed. Early in life she confessed Christ as her Savior; and by Bible study and prayer and gospel obedience, she sought to closely walk with God; and she dwelt among her own people, greatly

53

beloved by many, honored and respected by all,
fitted by social standing, by training, by native
gifts, and by rare personal influence to be a
leader; yet, withal, modest and self-distrusting,
she waited unconsciously for the call of the
Lord.

The writer of this Introduction, having had
perfect understanding of all things from the
very first pertaining to this "Crusade" work,
believes that he ought to say for Mrs. Thompson, and all the good women associated with
her in this undertaking, that they went out in
faith, not knowing whither they went; not
boldly, but modestly; not recklessly, but con-
sciously constrained of the Lord. They never
thought of the publicity and honor that future
years might bring them, but in a prayerful spirit
they tried to meet the present duty.

He also adds that some two or three weeks
after the "Crusade" began, it came to him as
an overpowering conviction that we were in the
beginning of a great movement, which would be
spoken of in future years like the "Reformation," or the religious movement in the time of
Wesley. He so publicly expressed himself then,
and has never seen any reason to reverse his
opinion.

These sketches of the "Crusade," written in
the quaint and readable style so characteristic

of Mrs. Thompson, are most heartily commended to the friends of temperance, and to its enemies as well, as an important contribution to the history of the temperance cause.

W. J. McSURELY,
Pastor Crusade Church.

PRESBYTERIAN PARSONAGE, }
   HILLSBORO, OHIO, 1894.   }

I.

VOLUMES have been written, and speeches without number made, setting forth most graphically the "Crusade of Woman against Rum." Yet strange to say, the call comes with greater and still greater earnestness to the leader of the little "band of seventy:" "Tell us more about the beginning of the Crusade in Hillsboro, and give us all the incidents connected with it, for the story must not die with the veterans of 1873 and 1874." As the shadows lengthen, and the number of that band counts fewer, I am reminded that what I do, I must do quickly.

Many years ago a friend wrote to me for a brief but plain account of the facts in connection with the starting of the Crusade in our town, and of my relation to it. Supposing at the time that it was for her own personal interest merely, I wrote freely, withholding no part of the truth as it occurred.

That narrative was adopted by Miss Willard in her work, "Woman and Temperance," and has become the "old, old story." After all these years I could not change the "facts and

57

figures," and might not change the diction to
profit; therefore, with slight additions, I furnish
it as the first of the promised series of Crusade
sketches from the "Old Fort."

On the evening of December 22, 1873, Dio
Lewis, a Boston physician and lyceum lecturer,
delivered in Music Hall, Hillsboro, Ohio, a
lecture on "Our Girls." He had been engaged
by the Lecture Association, some months before,
to fill one place in the winter course of lectures,
merely for the entertainment of the people; but
finding that he could remain another evening,
and still reach his next appointment (Washington Court-house), he consented to give another
lecture on the evening of the 23d. At the sug-
gestion of Judge Albert Matthews, an old-line
temperance man and Democrat, a free lecture
on temperance became the order of the evening.

Dr. Lewis was our guest until the morning
of the 23d, when my brother, Colonel Wm. H.
Trimble, took him to his beautiful "Woodland"
home, intending to send him across the country
to Washington Court-house in his own carriage
on the morning of the 24th.

I did not hear Dio Lewis lecture because of
home cares that required my presence; but my
son, a youth of seventeen, and my daughter
were there, and they came to me upon their return home, and in a most earnest manner related

the thrilling incidents of the evening; how Dr. Lewis told of his own mother, and several of her good Christian friends, uniting in prayer with and for the liquor-sellers of his native town, until they gave up their soul-destroying business. Dr. Lewis said, "Ladies, you might do the same thing in Hillsboro, if you had the same faith," and then turning to the ministers and temperance men who were upon the platform, added: "Suppose I ask the women of this audience to signify their opinions upon the subject?" They all bowed their consent, and fifty or more women stood up in token of approval. He then asked the men how many of them would stand as "backers," should the women undertake the work. Sixty or seventy arose. "And," continued my son, "you are on some committees to do work at the Presbyterian church in the morning, and the ladies expect you to go out with them to the saloons!"

My husband, who had returned from Adams County Court that evening and was feeling very tired, seemed asleep as he rested upon the sofa, while my children in an undertone had given me all the above facts; but as the last sentence was uttered, he raised himself up upon his elbow and said: "What tomfoolery is all that?" My dear children slipped out of the room quietly, and I betook myself to the task of consoling their

father, with the promise that I should not be led
into any foolish act by Dio Lewis, or any association of human beings, but added: "If the
Lord should show me that it was his will for the
women to visit places where liquors were sold
and drunk, I should not shrink from it."

After some time my husband relaxed into a
milder mood, continuing to call the whole plan,
as he understood it, "tomfoolery." I ventured
to remind him that the men had been in the
"tomfoolery" business a long time, and suggested that it might be God's will that the
women should now take their part.

Nothing farther was said upon the subject
until the next morning after breakfast. "Are
you going to the church this morning?" asked
the children. I hesitated, and doubtless showed
in my countenance the burden upon my spirit.
My husband walked the length of the room several times, and finally said: "Children, you know
where your mother goes to settle all vexed questions. Instead of family prayers this morning, let
her alone to make her decision." I went to my
room, kneeling before God and his Holy Word,
to see what would be sent me, when I heard a
step at the door, and upon opening it, my
daughter stood there. With tearful eyes she
handed me her small, open Bible and said with
with trembling voice: "See what my eyes fell

upon. It must be for you." She immediately
left the room, and I sat down to read the
wonderful message of the great "I Am" contained in the 146th Psalm. And as I read, new
meaning seemed to attach to those promises
(so often read before), and the Spirit said: "This
is the way, walk ye in it." No longer doubting,
I quickly repaired to the Presbyterian Church,
and took my seat near the door. Several of my
friends came, and urged me to go up to the front.
While hesitating, I was unanimously chosen as
president or leader, Mrs. General McDowell
vice-president, and Mrs. D. K. Fenner secretary
of the strange work that was to follow.

Appeals were drawn up to druggists, saloon-
keepers, and hotel proprietors. Then the pastor
of the Presbyterian Church, Rev. Dr. McSurely,
who had up to this time occupied the chair, called
upon the chairman-elect to "come forward to the
post of honor." But your humble servant could
not; her limbs refused to bear her. The dear
ladies offered me assistance, but it was not God's
time. My brother, Colonel Trimble, observing
my embarrassed situation, said to Dr. McSurely:
"I believe the ladies will do nothing until the
gentlemen of the audience leave the house!"

After some moments, Dr. McSurely said: "I
believe Colonel Trimble is right. Brethren, let

us adjourn, and leave this work with God and the women."

As the last man closed the door after him, strength before unknown came to me, and without any hesitation or consultation I walked forward to the minister's table, and opened the large Bible, explained the incidents of the morning; then read, and briefly (as my tears would allow) commented upon its new meaning to me.

I then called upon Mrs. McDowell to lead in prayer; and such a prayer! It seemed as though the angel had brought down "live coals" from off the altar and touched her lips—she who, by her own confession, had never before heard her own voice in prayer!

As we arose from our knees (for all were kneeling that morning), I asked Mrs. Cowden, the Methodist Episcopal minister's wife, a grand singer of the "olden style," to start my favorite hymn, "Give to the winds thy fears," to the familiar tune of St. Thomas, and turning to the dear women, I said: "As we all join in singing this hymn, let us form in line, two and two, and let us at once proceed to our sacred mission, trusting alone in the 'God of Jacob.'"

It was all done in less time than it takes to write it. Every heart was throbbing and every woman's countenance betrayed her solemn re-

alization of the fact that she was going "about her Father's business."

As this "band of mysterious beings" first encountered the outside gaze, and as they passed from the door of the old church and reached the street beyond the large churchyard, they were singing these prophetic words:

> "Far, far above thy thought
> His counsel shall appear,
> When fully He the work hath wrought ·
> That caused thy needless fear."

On we marched in solemn silence, looking neither to the right nor left, until we arrived at the drugstore of Dr. Wm. Smith on East Main Street. Mrs. Milton Boyd had been appointed to read "the appeal" on that morning, and proceeded to do so. From the minutes so carefully kept by our secretary, Mrs. D. K. Fenner, we extract the following:

"Dr. Wm. Smith, after much persuasion, signed the 'druggists pledge,' with the understanding that he, as a physician, had a right to prescribe liquor and sell on his own prescription.

"Seybert and Isaman signed very willingly, and assured the ladies of their good wishes.

"Mr. James Brown, Sr., signed also willingly.

"Mr. Wm. H. H. Dunn postponed his decision."

"HILLSBORO, OHIO, December 24, 1873.

Before entering upon the second chapter, I yield to the entreaty of many friends and insert my husband's first impressions of this memorable morning. The second chapter gives the story of the "Crusade Hymn," and why I chose it as our marching song.

Judge Thompson's account of this movement, taken from his History of the County of Highland: "The town of Hillsboro has always been noted for its interest in the encouragement of all systems of education, and few populations have excelled that of Hillsboro in the promotion of female education; the result of which has been to establish a high standard of refinement of both sexes, and an unusually independent order of thought and action between them, as is evidenced by the fact that the Woman's Temperance Crusade had its birth in the village, and has already breathed its infant breath throughout Christendom. Books have been written, voluminous reports have been made, and eloquent speeches have been uttered as to the minute details of the origin of the Woman's Temperance Crusade in Hillsboro, and most of them are true in statement and in fact; but nowhere has pen ventured a description of the band—the cohort, the troupe. No! rather the apparition of seventy women in sable black arrayed, and in settled line of march, moving as when first seen on the streets of Hillsboro.

"It was a dark, cloudy, cold, and still Decem-

ber day, no sun shining from above, no wind
playing around, a little snow leisurely dropping
down, and under the magic command of their
own leaders, chosen on the instant at the
hurried previous organization at the Presbyterian church, the procession moved with
solemn steps, as if each woman had been
trained for that day's work from the cradle.

'Not a drum was heard, not a funeral note,'

but the poetic mind instantly hummed the 'Ode
of Charles Wolfe at the Burial of Sir John
Moore.' Husbands saw their wives, sons and
daughters their mothers, and neighbors their
friends, moving along with the strange apparition, and knew not what it meant, until before
some liquor saloon or hotel or drugstore, you
could hear the singing of some familiar hymn
warble through the air in tones of the most
touching note; and then, solemn silence prevail-
ing up and down street, the utterance of a soul-
stirring prayer made by some lady, with all
others kneeling around on curbstone or pavement or door-sill, could be heard ascending to the
throne of God to avert the curse of intemperance.

"No crowd of shouting boys followed; no
cliques of consulting men on the street corners
were gathered; every countryman halted his
team in awe; no vociferous angry words were

5

heard, and no officer commanded the peace—
for it was death-like peace. Throughout the
day, songs and prayers were heard at all places
kept for the sale of liquors, and at night consultation was resumed at the church, from
whence the " Phœnix-like body," springing from
the ashes of the "funeral pyre" of woman's im-
molation, had emerged in the morning; and there,
in making reports, prayer, and singing in spirit
as never before, was sung on Christmas Eve:

> ' Ring out the grief that saps the mind,
>   For those that here we see no more;
>   Ring out the feud of rich and poor,
>   Ring in redress to all mankind.'

"They remained until the moon in the last
quarter lighted their pathway to homes, whose
inmates as spectators of the troupe when the
first curtain was raised, stood around the hearth-
stones in as much wonder as if a company of
celestial beings had on that day come down
from the skies.

"Such is a dim outline of the first parade of
the Woman's Temperance Crusade at Hillsboro;
and well may it be said of the 'opening of the
heavens' on that memorable day, that 'He who
made a decree for the rain and a way for the
lightning' will alone limit its effects on the na-
tions of the earth."

II.

STORY OF THE "CRUSADE HYMN."

WHEN David, "the stripling," essayed to go out against the vaunting "Goliath of Gath," his only reason for so daring a feat was that the God of Israel had in the past enabled him to kill both a lion and a bear. "And David said to Saul, the king of Israel," (whose approval he must have), "the Lord that delivered me out of the paw of the lion and out of the paw of the bear, he will deliver me out of the hand of this Philistine. . . . And Saul said unto David, Go, and the Lord be with thee."

Thus the inspiration of past experiences aided the earnest women in their new departure, and gave to their untrained leader fresh courage and faith, as she remembered how, in the "long ago," her heart had been taught to sing:

"Give to the winds thy fears."

Early in the winter of 1852, when our children numbered six, the eldest son away from home at school, and the youngest an infant of a few months, the scarlet fever became an epidemic in our town, and three of our dear children became victims to it.

About the same time a valued young woman,

who had been in the family for some years, was taken with quinsy, and was removed by her parents to their home, two miles in the country. Thus I was left with an infant, three children confined to their beds, and no assistance save a little colored girl about ten years of age, and a stable boy, who, by the way, knew everybody, and was able to serve us a good purpose in searching for needed help. In the evening, however, he returned after a fruitless quest, and reported: "Can't get nobody—all fear'd of dat 'zease." So I kept on, and provided for the various needs of my family as best I could, until my husband, who always had a very tender feeling for ladies who were oppressed with work (yet had no native tact to aid), devised a plan by which he might do me essential service. He mounted his horse, and started to the farm, three miles from town, trusting that the wife of the tenant might be induced to come to our rescue in such an emergency, as she had no children, and had once lived with us. But there was a stream to cross before reaching the farm, and it was frozen over. Regardless of the smooth shoes of his horse, he ventured, and lo! the noble horse fell, crushing the right leg of the rider. The sufferer was gently lifted by a stalwart farmer passing with his sled, laid upon the straw, the poor, limping horse tied to the hinder part; and so he was safely, but painfully, brought to our door.

The sight and the history would have done for me what "the last pound" did for the camel's back, but for the gratitude that came welling up in my heart that my poor husband's limb was not broken, neither was our noble family horse killed!

With such addition to my cares, however, it can well be supposed, after nine days and nights of weary, sleepless nursing and toiling, with no change for the better, my heart and strength began to fail, and I reasoned thus with myself about midnight: I have tried since a child to love the Savior; I have denied myself, taken up my cross, and made an honest effort to follow him—and now I am deserted, and in the town of my nativity I am forsaken! Quick as thought the enemy said: "I'll tell you what to do: leave the Church; for you are a hypocrite if you keep your name there, feeling as you do."

I at once laid my sleeping infant in its cradle, determined to act promptly, and write a note to our Methodist minister. As I arose to do so, an inward voice seemed to say, "Open that hymn-book first;" and as I looked around, the old book of songs was taken from its place, and carelessly opened, without design or hope on my part, show-

ing that it was all of love and pity that John
Wesley's hymn, "Give to the winds thy fears,"
was the one that first met my gaze, and caused
the instant and complete transformation that followed.   Taking a seat by the cradle, the emotions
of my heart found utterance in the song of songs,
" How firm a foundation, ye saints of the Lord !"
and forgetting that the poor patients might be
aroused, one verse after another was sung, sweeter
than ever before it seemed, until from the adjoining room my husband called out, "Eliza,
what do you find to sing about?"

I said : "I am singing about our holy religion."   He reached out his hands to me :

" Wife, I know you are an honest woman;
now, tell me, do you find anything in your religion to comfort you—situated as you now are?"

I answered him honestly that I had never felt
happier in my life!   With a firm grasp of my
hand, he said, emphatically: " Then I must
seek it!"

Thus had the "Comforter" not only enabled
me to "give to the winds my fears," but had
taught my anxious heart to

> Leave to His sov'reign sway
> To choose and to command,"

in the work which had hitherto caused my
greatest care.   Can it be wondered that this

blessed hymn, with all its sacred influences, should come to my mind when we were about to step out upon an untried way, and venture across the line of public sentiment—all helpless, save in the strength which God supplies?

But this is not all. No one could be found who was willing, for "love or money," to risk the "plague" and do a day's washing; therefore an airy place had been prepared, our unwashed clothes had been assorted and disinfected, and we were trusting and waiting. Good Katharine had recovered, and had come as an angel of mercy to sit with the children and thus relieve me for other work.

The crisis of the disease had passed safely with our dear little ones, and our hearts were full of gratitude. The winter seemed gone, for "the singing of birds had come, and the voice of the turtle was heard in the land." New courage took possession of our souls, and although the last word of "kindly command" from my husband—recovered from his lameness, and on the way to county court— as he drove off was, "See that a bonfire is made of the soiled clothes, below the barn," other plans were in the head of the one who had put so many careful stitches into those little garments; therefore, "with malice toward none," as soon as he was out of sight, "John, the faithful," was quietly directed to make a fire in the laundry furnace, and fill the boilers. Then, as poor, blind Samson cried to God for strength "this once," before taking hold of the pillars, so did I implore the evidence of strength before acting upon my own judgment.

Well, the answer of approval came, and by two o'clock my clothes-lines in the back lawn were filled with snowy garments and household linen, and I felt none the worse! While poor John, with few words but a fixed expression of amazement, put all things in order for me. A nice appetizing dinner was then prepared for the delicate part of the family, and a hearty one for the laborers. Surely, I could never doubt the promise: "As thy days, so shall thy strength be."

In all this I feared nothing so much as the criticism of my dear father, who came over each day to inquire for the sick and to care for our temporal wants—my good mother being quite unable to leave her room. As the dear old gentleman rode up, I cautioned the grown ones of the nursery to keep quiet; but his keen eye spied the large washing upon the lines, and at once congratulated me upon having found a laundress. The smiles that passed told the tale, and with a most reproving look at his only daughter, he said: "My child, I am surprised at you." But with a forgiving kiss, he only added: "It is

useless to ask you to take care of yourself."
And surely he would have been confirmed in his
opinion had he lived to witness the Crusade of
1873 and 1874; but his noble heart would have
been with us.

III.

STORY OF SALOON VISITATION.

AT the time of the "new departure" on the
part of the ladies of Hillsboro, there were
four hotels, four drugstores, and thirteen saloons
where intoxicating liquors could be obtained,
there being little hindrance, save the conscien-
tious scruples of individual cases!

When the "Praying Band," as it was called
in ridicule, first started out upon its divinely-
appointed mission, as the procession of somber-
looking beings passed up High Street from the
church where their first meeting of consecration
had just been held, Dr. Dio Lewis was driven
slowly by on his way from Colonel Trimble's
home to Washington Court-house.

On the following morning, the 25th, many of
the earnest women and quite a goodly number
of zealous brethren assembled promptly at nine
o'clock in the Presbyterian church to renew their
consecration vows. After a season of fervent

prayer, song, and testimony, it was voted to respect a previous appointment for religious services in the Episcopal church—quite a number of our band being members of that Church, and their rector, Rev. John Ely, one of our loyal supporters. It was also thought wise to give to our families the attention due the established usage of Christmas-day. Therefore, after adjournment, an informal prayer-meeting was held, which strengthened the hearts of all greatly, and better prepared the women for the services of the following morning.

The cold, clear, crisp morning of the 26th dawned upon us with a sparkling snow upon the ground, but paths were shoveled and swept by new hands that morning, and, as we passed, heads were uncovered and earnest benedictions showered upon us by many a manly heart, which dared to be on the right side. The nine o'clock prayer-meeting was opened by Scripture reading, prayer, and song; earnest exhortations and words of hearty support and encouragement were offered by Dr. McSurely and others.

The Committee of Visitation, after singing a hymn, adjourned to meet at the same time and place the next morning; then, forming in procession, it visited hotels and saloons in the following order—quoting from minutes:

"Mrs. Thompson was appointed to present

appeal at hotels and saloons." "The first call
was made at the Uhrig saloon, on East High
Street. There we were met by smooth words and
fair promises, but no signatures." "Kramer House
proprietor—*not at home.*" "Ellicott House—the
polite landlord said he did hope we would suc-
ceed, but could not close his bar unless the others
would." "The kind proprietor of the Woodrow
House half agreed to give up the miserable business, and said he certainly would if the other
hotels of the town would close up."

It was quite evident to the minds of the
ladies that the question with these gentlemen
turned upon the pivot of popularity and financial success, and not upon any innate love of
the curse, for the fact was too apparent that
the effects of liquor-drinking had proven the
hardest part of a landlord's office.

Fortified with hope in the evident unrest of
these men, who were building upon sandy
foundations—their hope of gain—our next call
was at the saloon of John Bales. He was cool
and polite, treated the subject-matter of our visit
in a purely business way, proposed selling out
his entire stock, billiard tables and all, at two-
thirds of invoiced value, and *sell no more liquor!*
As this was quite out of the line of our warfare
against spiritual wickedness in high places, we
turned our faces towards the first-class saloon

(as it was called) kept by Robert Ward, on High Street, a resort made famous by deeds, the memory of which nerved the heart and paled the cheek of some among us, as the seventy entered the open door of the "witty Englishman" (as his patrons were wont to call the popular Ward). Doubtless he had learned of our approach, as he not only propped the heavy door open, but with the most perfect suavity of manner held it until the ladies all passed in; then, closing it, walked to his accustomed stand behind the bar.

Seizing the strange opportunity, the leader addressed him as follows: "Well, Mr. Ward, this must seem to you a strange audience! I suppose, however, that you understand the object of our visit?" "Robert" by this time began to perspire freely, and remarked that he would like to have a talk with Dio Lewis. Mrs. Thompson said: "Dr. Lewis has nothing whatever to do with the subject of our mission. As you look upon some of the faces before you, and observe the marks of sorrow, caused by the unholy business that you ply, you will find that it is no wonder we are here. We have come, however, not to threaten, not even to upbraid, but in the name of our Divine Friend and Savior, and in his spirit, to forgive, and to commend you to his pardon, if you will but agree to abandon a business that is so damaging to our hearts and to the peace of our homes!"

The hesitation and embarrassment of the famous saloon-keeper seemed to afford (as the leader thought) an opportunity for prayer; so, casting her eye around upon that never-to-be-forgotten group of earnest faces, she said, *very softly:* "Let us pray." Instantly all, even the poor liquor-seller himself, were upon their knees, Mrs. McSurely, wife of the Presbyterian minister. was asked by Mrs. Thompson to lead in prayer, but she declined. The spirit of utterance then came upon the latter, and, as a seal of God's approval upon the self-sacrificing work there inaugurated, the Holy Spirit touched all hearts. As we arose from our knees, dear Mrs. Doggett (now in heaven) broke forth in her sweet, pathetic notes, and all joined with her in singing:

> "There is a fountain filled with blood,
>   Drawn from Immanuel's veins;
>   And sinners plunged beneath that flood,
>   Lose all their guilty stains."

The scene that followed, in a most remarkable manner portrayed the spirit of our holy religion. Poor wives and mothers, who the day before would have crossed the street to avoid passing by a place so identified with their heartaches, their woes, and their deepest humiliation, in tearful pathos were now pleading with this deluded brother to accept the world's Redeemer as his own. Surely, "God is Love!"

Shortly after the ladies retired from this their first saloon prayer-meeting, a message from Dr. Lewis, at Washington Court-house, was received by Colonel William H. Trimble to this effect: " The women over here are terribly in earnest." As the report of union in this strange work first greeted our ears and strengthened our hearts, " Praise ye the Lord" seemed more and more a fitting prelude to our " Magna Charta"—the 146th Psalm—and we entered upon the Saturday morning prayer service with renewed faith and courage.

Dr. Mathews, president of the Hillsboro Female College, the renowned and venerated educator of woman in our community for so many years, presided over the meeting, and spoke to our hearts such words of earnest commendation and sympathy that the "doubting ones" could but have been convinced as was Thomas of old.

William H. H. Dunn, the druggist, who was not at his place of business on the morning of the visit by the " band of ladies," sent in his reply to their "appeal." It read as follows:

" LADIES,—In compliance with my agreement I give you this promise, that I will carry on my business in the future as I have in the past; that is to say, that in the sale of intoxicating liquors I will comply with the law, nor will I sell to any person whose father, mother, wife, or daughter send me a written request not to make such sale."

There was some discussion as to whether Mr. Dunn's pledge should be received as satisfactory. Remarks were made by the gentlemen as well as the ladies, but it was soon apparent that there were mothers in that audience who could never vote to have "his business" carried on "in the future as in the past." Action was therefore deferred.

Next in order came a message from Mr. Bennet, the master of the Hillsboro Grange: "Say to the ladies for me, *God bless them;* and, poor man that I am, I will back them with fifty dollars if it is needed."

It was resolved at this Saturday morning meeting to hold a mass temperance-meeting in the Methodist Episcopal Church on Sunday evening, December 28th, and a committee of three ministers—Rev. Dr. McSurely, of the Presbyterian Church; Rev. Mr. Cowden, of the Methodist; and Rev. John Ely, of the Episcopal Church— were chosen to take charge of said meeting, inviting both ladies and gentlemen to speak. Rev. Mr. Ely was also requested to invite Father Donahue, of the Catholic Church, and his temperance society, to join us in our work.

After uniting in a fervent prayer and singing part of a favorite hymn, the committee adjourned to meet on Monday morning, at the same time and place. Procession then formed, and visits were made at two hotels and three saloons. One of the saloon-keepers expressed a great desire to *get out of the business.* With this encouraging prospect we ended the first week of the "Crusade" in Hillsboro.

IV.

HILLSBORO CRUSADE SKETCHES.

DECEMBER 27, 1873, we find recorded on the minutes of our "Woman's Temperance League," the first desire expressed on the part of a liquor-dealer of Hillsboro "to quit the business." In a few days after that, two others manifested a willingness to *be relieved!* The ways and means were under consideration, and well-chosen committees were quietly intrusted with the cases.

In the meantime, the morning prayer-meetings were continued with increasing interest. The daily visitations of the band, now numbering over eighty, to "all places where liquors were sold and drunk on the premises" were faithfully kept up. The mass-meeting in Music Hall, or

in the Methodist Episcopal church, several evenings of each week, were always well attended and
of great interest to the public, as reports were
made there by the zealous workers of incidents
"along the weary way," and the speeches, prayers, and songs were of that enthusiastic order
peculiar to the times.

January 3d, the morning prayer service was
of a most impressive nature. The committee
which had been appointed to present the " Physician's Pledge," Mrs. McSurely, Mrs. Thomas
Barry, Mrs. Jessie K. Pickering, Mrs. James Patterson, Mrs. William Barry, reported as follows :
" Found the County Medical Convention in session; were presented to the Convention and politely received." The object of the visit being
made known, the physicians there present signed
an approved physician's pledge to the number of
seventeen of Highland County's best-known physicians.

This was received with thanksgiving, as those
intrusted with the care of families know too well
the fearful risk of intoxicating prescriptions from
the family doctor, not to appreciate the value of
such a victory.

When the hour for business had passed, and
the usual visiting ordeal was in order, the ladies
were most agreeably surprised by the announce-
ment that they would be expected to call upon

6

Colonel Cook to express their thanks that he had closed the bar of the "Ellicott House." After singing, with an unusual amount of zeal, "Praise God, from whom all blessings flow," the procession formed, and at once proceeded to make this visit. The ladies were politely met by the genial landlord and his kindly wife, and ushered into the spacious parlor of this old and popular hotel.

During the conversation that followed, the colonel complained that the temperance public had not stood by him, when, on a former occasion, he had closed his bar, but patronized hotel where liquors were sold.

The leader of the band, feeling the embarrassment of the situation, proposed that all should unite in prayer that the temperance people "stand by their colors," and with heart and soul sustain their brother in his effort for the right. It was most natural that an earnest petition should be added for the proprietor, who was bravely facing the losses as well as the crosses of the situation. Blessings from full hearts were invoked upon the colonel, his wife, and his house, and as that honest prayer was ended, all joined in a sweet song of thanksgiving, and parted with the most cordial good feeling.

The Visiting Committee proceeded to call upon the other hotels that morning, to secure, if possible, the consent of the proprietors to close their bars on the approaching stock-sale day. Saloons were also appealed to upon the subject. Some consented; others promised to *be very careful* in their sales! Our secretary furnished the following facts after the sale-day was over:

" The result of the day's work was most satisfactory. There was less drunkenness on the streets than had ever before been known on a stock-sale day; indeed, almost *none at all!*"

Some matters of business were looked into pertaining to the charitable feature of our work. Then it was determined to appoint a committee of three ladies to report to Mr. Dunn that the Woman's Temperance Association could not conscientiously agree to his last proposed " druggist's pledge;" but instructions were given to this committee of Christian ladies—Mrs. Judge Evans, Mrs. Pickering, and Mrs. Nelson—to convey to Mr. Dunn the good wishes of our Society, with the sincere desire that he would agree to the uniform druggist pledge, and thus remove one of the greatest stumbling-blocks out of the way of our success in this community.

The band, after singing most feelingly the hymn so expressive of their convictions that morning,—

> "Must Jesus bear the cross alone,
> And all the world go free?
> No, there's a cross for every one,
> And there's a cross for me,"—

took up with renewed courage the sacred cross, and proceeded to their work of visitation.

Passing along Main Street, west of High, on that cold, snowy January morning, a sign, hitherto unobserved by the band, appeared in view. It read, "The Lava Bed;" it was in the basement of a large business house; the proprietor's name was Joseph Lance. It only required a moment's reflection, and, led by the regular officers of the band, they descended the steep, snowy, stone steps to hold a prayer and song service on the sawdust floor of that low-down saloon! It was literally a low-down saloon, but the women recognized the fact that Joe Lance had a soul to be saved from the woe of making his neighbor drunken; so they felt constrained to give him their prayers and songs, their Scripture readings and their persuasion, just as they had given them to those nearer the light of heaven, who were engaged in the same business. The poor fellow was taken by surprise, but was kind and respectful, and after the ladies left had "strange thoughts," as he afterwards confessed.

Reports were now coming in from many quarters of the wonderful success of this "woman's movement," as it was called, and many who had been faithless were now saying: "It must be of God!" Messages from our association to Wilmington, New Vienna, Greenfield, and other

places, were sent, and from them to us in return,
until it really did seem that a chain of love for
God and humanity was about to bind the hearts
of Christians together for royal service for the
Master! And although after twenty years we
may well sing:

> "It may not be my way,
> It may not be thy way,
> And yet, in his own way,
> The Lord will provide "—

as,

> "Bands of ribbon white,
> Around the world!"

do witness.

V.

ONE of the most remarkable features of the
"Woman's Temperance Movement" was
the rapidity with which the fire of enthusiasm
spread; and another was the spirit of zeal and
self-abnegation that seemed to take possession
of the best and most useful women in communities touched by this fire. We learn from recorded history that "in less than two weeks
from the time it was inaugurated at Hillsboro
three or four counties in Southern Ohio were
taken by storm!"

A reporter of the Cincinnati *Commercial* says
(January, 1874): "The excitement pervading the

entire community over the 'Woman's Temperance Movement' exceeds anything we have witnessed in Hillsboro during a residence of twenty years. And yet, on the part of the women engaged in it—despite old prejudices and present discouragements—a spirit of courageous faith and earnest prayer, added to a most forgiving disposition towards those whose business they especially antagonized, seems to characterize the movement wherever developed."

On the morning of January 12th, our early services were conducted by Dr. McSurely in the Presbyterian church, and his words and faithful Bible readings (always good) were so fitly spoken that they were indeed "like apples of gold in pictures of silver." Business of much interest followed. First, General McDowell said he had been requested to state to the meeting that the hotel-keepers wished a committee of gentlemen to be sent to confer with them in regard to "this movement," and to receive their proposals. It was "moved and carried" that the ladies vote on this request, and the request was granted.

The following gentlemen—Mr. F. I. Bumgarner, Mr. J. M. Boyd, General J. J. McDowell, Mr. M. T. Nelson, and Mr. Samuel E. Hibben—were appointed to wait upon the hotel-keepers as a committee of conference. The men in charge of aiding the business houses who wished to reship their liquors to Cincinnati reported the readiness of two firms to accept terms and quit the business. The ladies, true to their promise, signified their intention of meeting at an appointed time for the purchase of candies, glasses, beer-mugs, etc., and thus aid the parties to start in a more desirable occupation.

A message was sent in by one or two of the hotel-keepers, through Mr. Samuel E. Hibben, requesting that the following ladies be added to the committee of gentlemen appointed to confer with them: Mesdames Colonel Trimble, William Scott, Jessie K. Pickering, Judge Evans, and E. J. Thompson. The society indorsed the request. A message announcing the pleasant news that our Washington Court-house friends would be with us that evening was received with evidences of delight.

A committee was also appointed to invite town, county, and United States officers to attend the meetings of the Woman's Temperance Association. Meeting adjourned with the benediction, and the ladies formed in procession and made several visits to saloons, inviting all to come out and hear from our Washington Court-house friends.

The mass-meeting in the evening was large and enthusiastic, with addresses by "Mr. Morehouse, the superintendent of schools, and Mr.

Dean, teacher of high school" of that place. They gave accounts of the work there to the delight of all interested, although many of us felt heavy about the heart because of the "stones" that were not yet "rolled away" in our community.

An unusually large number of men and women assembled in the Presbyterian church at an early hour on the morning of the 13th of January, 1874. The regular order of business was set aside that the audience might hear from the visitors from Washington Court-house—that fortunate little city whose "liquor-sellers" all gave up to the prayers and entreaties of the good women, two of whom, Mrs. Carpenter and Mrs. Pruddy, gave us some words of encouragement. After adjournment, the ladies of the band went out for "visitations," found some doors *closed*, and our dealers *hard* and *unrelenting*, because they were fortified against the "Washington Court-house women," whom they expected with us! The men's prayer-meeting continued in session at the church, and the bell was rung at the end of every prayer.

About this time there was much feeling with regard to Mr. Dunn's course toward the ladies and their reasonable wishes. Without consulting them, our highly-esteemed friend, Rev. J. McD. Mathews, aided by the man whom all society delighted to honor, Mr. Samuel E. Hibben, decided to secure the names of prominent business and professional men of the community to a personal appeal, and present it to Mr. Dunn. Over two hundred names were secured, and in the most kindly manner these two good men presented an appeal, and received from his attorneys his reply.

VI.

IT must "needs be" that much of interest is passed over in silence as we attempt a report of Crusade incidents. So varied and unique were the duties and thrilling occurrences of each day that of "making many books there would be no end," if all were told.

The following appeal, signed by about two hundred male citizens, had been presented to Mr. Dunn, the druggist, at the request of the temperance people, by a committee consisting of Rev. J. McD. Mathews and Mr. S. E. Hibben:

APPEAL.

MR. W. H. H. DUNN:

Dear Sir,—We, the undersigned citizens and business men of Hillsboro, would respectfully and kindly ask you to sign the "Women's Temperance Druggist's Pledge." We appeal to you as interested with us in the good name and prosperity of our town, and in view of the fact that some of our saloon-keepers are trying to make you their covering. We address you in no spirit of coercion, but as your neighbors and friends, who would have you with us in this temperance movement.

Should you decide to adopt the course here suggested, you will entitle yourself to our gratitude, as well as subserve, in our judgment, your own interests.

The subjoined reply was received at the hands of Mr. Dunn's attorneys:

MR. DUNN'S REPLY.

To Hon. Samuel E. Hibben and Rev. J. McD. Mathews:

Gentlemen,—Mr. W. H. H. Dunn, our client, to whom you presented a petition, signed by certain citizens of Hillsboro, requesting him to sign the "Women's Temperance Druggist's Pledge," bids us answer thus:

He is unable to see any difference between the request made in the petition referred to and the request originally presented by the ladies. He saw fit to refuse such request then, and sees no reason now to change his mind.

The "movement" forced him into the courts, and consequently placed him in direct antagonism with the temperance people connected with such "movement."

Until such a request as the one referred to is accompanied by proper concessions to him on the part of such temperance people, he can scarcely honor it with respectful or serious attention.

We beg leave to subscribe ourselves, very respectfully yours,   BEESON & SLOANE,
                                                                    COLLINS & PARKER.

It was a very singular pleasure that our band enjoyed on the morning of the 17th of January,

1874, to pass out of the church in a body, after the morning services were concluded, singing (in our hearts) that old gospel hymn,—

"Help us to help each other, Lord,
    Each other's cross to bear;
Let each his friendly aid afford,
    And feel his brother's care,"—

then to go where we believed a man was *honestly* making an effort to get out of a business so fraught with disastrous results to all concerned. When we arrived at the "Bank Saloon," we found our committee of temperance men finishing their part of the work of reshipments. They kindly proffered their aid, *and the auction commenced*, which resulted in each woman possessing a *trophy*, and Mr. Koch a full purse and an empty house, ready for (as we had hoped and prayed) a successful shoe-trade, as that was his original business. The pledge was presented to Mr. Koch, and from our minutes it seems he signed it with the added clause, "never to engage *in the business* in Hillsboro, Highland County, Ohio."

The women of the Association were most pleasantly surprised, at the evening meeting in the Presbyterian Church, to find themselves presented with two large and beautifully illuminated text-cards from Captain Amen, one to be

hung in the Presbyterian Church, and the other
in the Methodist. The texts were,

"In union there is strength."
"God's work pays sure wages."

It was moved (and seconded by Dr. Fullerton)
and carried, that Dr. Fullerton be requested to
frame these mottoes at his own expense. It
was no sooner said than done, and those embel-
lished cards, with their inspiring texts, and the
kindly thought on the path of our "weary way,"
gave the band much good cheer.

One morning about this time, as our ladies
were engaged in a song and prayer service in one
of the saloons, a message was received from our
friend of the "Lava Bed," who had not been forgotten or neglected. A conference was soon arranged with a committee of ladies, and Mr. Lance
made known his situation and his wishes. Plans
were immediately formed for the poor fellow's
relief from the heavy penalties resting upon him,
and Joseph found himself a free man, selling
fresh fish from a fine business stand, giving
strength, not "muddle," to human brains, and
peace to his own conscience.

It is needless to say that "fish, fresh fish,"
became the popular dish in the homes of the
Crusaders (as they were beginning to be called).

and our new "importer" for a time did a flourishing business.

Mr. Wm. Swartz, of the Jefferson House, now demanded attention. He was only a temporary actor in the saloon connected with the hotel, the property belonging to his widowed sister, Mrs. Liber. Mr. Swartz and his wife had tastes differing from that sort of life; hence it was not a very difficult task to persuade them to withdraw from it. Terms were agreed upon, and after the reshipment of liquors to Cincinnati, and the auction of beer-mugs, etc., Mr. Swartz found himself behind the counter of a flourishing grocery, and his little family enjoying the peace of an honest home without the "trail of the serpent."

News still reaching us of other localities coming under the influence of this marvelous "baptism of the Spirit," our hearts were being enlarged for further service, and communications of cordial sympathy were now of frequent occurrence.

VII.

THE DRUGSTORE-DAY.

SATURDAY morning, January 24, 1874, was a morning long to be remembered. After devotional services of more than usual interest and power, the women of the band, numbering about eighty, sallied forth from the dear old church that witnessed their first consecration, to encounter the piercing blasts of nature's cold, but more to feel the sting of malicious persecution, and witness the frowns of former friends, as they gathered in front of the "Palace Drugstore" for an all-day service of prayer and song.

It may be well to give our readers an idea of this day's work from an outsider's impression of it, as given in an organ of the Baptist Church, the *Watchman and Reflector*, of Boston. The editor prefaces the narrative by saying:

"If any think this is a work to be sneered at, let them read the following report of the efforts in Hillsboro, O., where the work began with a lecture by Dr. Lewis, on December 23, 1873. We confess we did not read it with dry eyes:

"Turning the corner on last Saturday afternoon, I came unexpectedly upon some fifty women kneeling on the pavement and stone steps before a store. . . . A daughter of a former governor of Ohio was leading in prayer. Surrounding her were the mothers, wives, and daughters of former congressmen and legislators, of lawyers, physicians, bankers, ministers, leading men of all kinds. . . . There were gathered here representatives from nearly every household of the town. The day was bitterly cold; a cutting north wind swept the streets, piercing us all to the bone. The plaintive, tender, earnest tones of that wife and mother who was pleading in prayer, arose on the blast, and were carried to every heart within reach. Passers-by uncovered their heads,

for the place whereon they trod was 'holy ground.'
The eyes of hardened men filled with tears, and many
turned away, saying that they could not bear to look
upon such a sight. Then the voice of prayer was
hushed; the women arose and began to sing, softly, a
sweet hymn with some old, familiar words and tune,
such as our mothers sang to us in childhood days. We
thought, Can mortal man resist such efforts? Then
they knelt, and once more the earnest tones of prayer
were borne upon the breeze. So, from ten o'clock in
the morning to four in the afternoon, the work went on,
the ladies relieving each other by relays.

"Close by was the residence of Hon. John A. Smith,
our former congressman, and now delegate to the Congressional Convention. His noble, warm-hearted wife,
one of the band, provided a bounteous lunch, to which the
workers resorted for rest and refreshment, then returned
to kneel and pray. The effect upon the spectators was
indescribable. No sneer was heard, scarcely a light
word was spoken. The spirit of devotion was abroad;
those who would scorn to pray themselves, yet felt that
here was something which they must, at least, respect.
Many a 'God bless them!' fell from lips accustomed to
use the name of Deity only in blasphemy. There was
not a man who saw them kneeling there, but felt that if
he was entering heaven's gate, and one of these women
were to approach, he would stand aside and let her enter first.

"The end is not yet; the hearts of these women daily
grow stouter, their faith brighter, and their prayers
more earnest. A thoroughly Christian spirit pervades
the community, and the feeling is one of yearning love
and pity for those who stand out against their duty to
their fellow-men."

A large and enthusiastic "mass temperance-meeting" was held in Music Hall on that Saturday evening, addressed by Rev. A. C. Hirst, of Washington Court-house. Subscriptions were then received to the Guarantee Fund, raising the amount to $12,000. The total-abstinence pledge was circulated (as was our habit at all public meetings), and many signatures obtained.

As the women retired from Music Hall that evening, in their hearts came welling up, "One more day's work for Jesus;" then the blessed promise, "They that suffer with me shall reign with me."

VIII.

AFTER the all-day services of the band in front of the Palace Drugstore on that memorable Saturday, the hospitable and refreshing luncheon at the home of our friends, Hon. and Mrs. John A. Smith, the eloquent address of Rev. A. C. Hirst in the evening at Music Hall, and a restful Sunday and spiritual upbuilding, the Monday morning meeting, January 26th, opened with new interest, and messages of fresh victories were received from many points.

Reports also came of the cruel and unmanly treatment the New Vienna women were receiving at the hands of Van Pelt, the notorious sa-

loonist. Words of earnest sympathy were sent
them from our association, and our hearts were
full of gratitude that we were spared such indig-
nities; and yet the stubborn resistance of some
with whom we had been pleading so prayerfully,
was, we thought, harder to bear than a shower
of sour beer and threats of violence! But God,
who alone can "temper the winds to the shorn
lamb," knew that the fathers, husbands, brothers
of Hillsboro could not have ruled their spirits as
did the quiet representatives of William Penn at
New Vienna, leaving the combat with "God and
the women."

Calls from the towns and hamlets of our own
and adjoining counties came almost daily for
help in their work, and willing hearts were always ready to respond. Indeed, the enthusiasm
was so high that our liverymen caught the in-
fection, many times furnishing carriages, horses,
and drivers for these rural missionary excursions.

About this time, January 28th, news came of
Springfield, Ohio, falling into line. Mother
Stewart, that grand, earnest woman, whom the
"Boys in Blue," with their tears of gratitude,
had christened "mother," for many years had
toiled for "God and humanity" in the temperance field, gaining cases under the Adair Law,
and pleading for poor, oppressed women and
children, who, because of the curse in the cup,

7

were cold and starving,—she now laid hold of the "spiritual lever" presented in the new method, although it was not thought a work adapted to cities. But of her success and her many fields of labor on this and on the other side of the sea, let her own book, "Memories of the Crusade," tell more at length than a local sketch permits.

The early prayer-meeting on the morning of the 26th was led by Rev. S. D. Clayton. Many interesting incidents of the work in Wilmington and other places were related by him, who was always an inspiration to us. There being no other business of importance after the devotional hour, the ladies in private session determined to spend the day in visitations upon the few remaining places that were selling liquors without restraint.

While the band was engaged in the usual services in front of the unrelenting druggist's, a man from the country, a farmer, strolled along the street, and when the voice of song arrested his attention, he stopped, and leaned against the wall of a building adjoining the one before which the ladies were grouped. When the song so familiar to his ears (for he had heard it in his boyhood home) died away, and the women kneeled, he removed his hat, folded his arms, and reverently listened. When they arose from prayer, and again com-

menced a low, sweet hymn, he rushed across the
street, and, meeting an old friend, grasped his
hand, saying: "I have taken my last drink! I
never felt before what a wrong the cursed habit
was to poor women."

That friend, a most reliable Christian gentleman, told me the incident several years since,
and added: "That man had been a tippler from
his youth, and for years past rarely came to town
and left sober; but since that day he has been a
total abstainer." He is now over eighty, a kind,
good man. His wife and family are happy, and
he never fails to bless the "Praying Band." Thus,
while this "whirlwind of the Lord" was "to
the Jews a stumbling-block, and to the Greeks
foolishness," it was to many "the power of God
and the wisdom of God."

Many such incidents could be related, to off-
set the ridicule heaped upon the self-sacrificing women of those trying days; but God will
"avenge his own elect, who cry unto him day
and night, though he bear long" with their op-
pressors!

On Saturday morning, January 31st, after the
usual devotional services in the Presbyterian
Church, the members of the Association, having
been notified not to have singing and prayer at
the door or on the steps and pavement in front
of Mr. Dunn's drugstore, there was some dis-

cussion as to the best course of action. It was finally decided that the ladies should go out as usual visiting other places first. A committee of three was then appointed to request permission from the mayor to have a tent erected in the street in front of Mr. Dunn's store, outside the curbing. This committee was Mesdames William Trimble, John A. Smith, William Scott. A committee of gentlemen was then appointed to erect the said tent. The committee was Messrs. Jacob Sayler, F. Shepherd, J. S. Black, Allen Cooper, Pangburn, Roe, Duffey.

Permission having been obtained, the committee proceeded to erect the tabernacle; and later in the day, the band, having completed other work, took possession, and remained during the afternoon, for devotional services. Mrs. D. K. Fenner, our secretary (and she was a dignified Episcopalian), records in her minutes: "Few that were present will ever forget that scene, or the feelings of holy courage and faith that animated each heart."

Mr. Dunn now determined to call the law to his aid, securing the services of the lawyer who had antagonized the Washington Court-house ladies in the "Charlie Beck" case. Judge Safford, whose term on the bench had nearly expired, and whose sympathies were far from being with the temperance women (or men), was appealed to by

William H. H. Dunn and his lawyer for a temporary injunction. It was granted, and the notice
served upon the chairman of the Tabernacle
Committee, Mr. Sayler. In the dead hour of the
night the structure was taken down by our law-
abiding brethren of the committee, and when
Sunday dawned not a trace of the tent remained.

But what did the God of Jacob say to the
women who were trusting in him? Even as he
had, through the Spirit's guidance, shown in the
one hundred and forty-sixth Psalm to them in
the beginning of their mission, so now, words of
reassurance came to the heart of their leader
through the first chapter of Nahum, beginning
with the seventh verse: "The Lord is good, a
stronghold in the day of trouble, and he knoweth
them that trust in him. But with an overrun-
ning flood he will make an utter end of the place
thereof, and darkness shall pursue his enemies."
The entire chapter was applied with great comfort and strong faith, even to the last verse:
"Keep thy solemn feasts, perform thy vows."

On the Monday morning following, February
2d, by previous appointment, the Association met
in the Presbyterian Church for devotional services. A mass-meeting for the following Saturday
was determined upon, invitations to be sent to
our friends throughout the county, and a special
one, with our heartfelt congratulations, to the

faithful sisters of New Vienna, and Rev. D. Hill, of the Friends' Church, was invited to speak at the hall in the afternoon, with a request that he should bring Van Pelt with him, if it was really true (as we had heard) that he had not only given up the "evil of his doings," but had taken upon himself allegiance to the cause of temperance and humanity. But so grievous had been his persecutions of the temperance women that, as with the disciples of old, Saul "was feared," until he proved that "the scales had fallen from his eyes."

IX.

THE ladies of the Temperance Association of Hillsboro had very little to do with the legal proceedings connected with the injunction granted by Judge Safford against the Association, "restraining them from praying and singing around, before, or anywhere in the vicinity of Mr. William H. H. Dunn's drugstore." 'T is true quite a number of matrons (about thirty) assembled at the residence of the secretary, Mrs. Dean K. Fenner, by request of their lawyers, Messrs. Harrion, Williams, and Thompson, for conversation upon the subject in litigation. Mr. Thompson a day or two later met the members

of the Association in the lecture-room of the
Methodist Episcopal church and read to them
the affidavit, which they signed and swore to in
the presence of 'Squire Doggett.

When the day arrived for the hearing of the
case the "lady defendants," to the number of
about one hundred—our band had increased
during these days of persecution—formed in procession, after an early prayer-meeting at the
Methodist Episcopal church, and marched down
High Street to the court-house. We were received courteously and seated, although the court-
room was densely packed. The greatest interest
was manifested in the extraordinary proceedings,
and temperance sentiment was created, even
more rapidly by our court-house experiences
than by our saloon visitations; so the world
said.

The case was argued for four days, with great
skill and much feeling on both sides, during which
the most intense interest was shown by the people
from the rural districts as well as by our own citizens. Finally, the case was concluded, and Judge
Steel gave his decision. "The temporary injunction was dissolved, but only on a technicality,
and not on the merits of the case." Both parties were disappointed, and throughout the State
there was much feeling evinced on the part of
temperance advocates because of the fact that

this decision gave to many localities an assurance of the law on the liquor side, so that efforts were made in many towns in Ohio, where the movement was in progress, to put a check upon it in the same way. But, thank the good Father of all our mercies, the courts were generally in sympathy with the ladies. Judge after judge was appealed to in vain. In Morrow serious hindrance was suffered on the part of the temperance people because of the restraining orders of courts; but through the decision of Judge Smith, of Lebanon, all honor to his name, the women triumphed in the only injunction case of the Crusade that was decided on its merits. Without entering into the arguments upon which his decision was based, let it be remembered that the pivot upon which all arguments turned with that good, wise, common-sense judge was that "the plaintiff had no right to ask legal protection for a manifestly illegal business."

Soon after the new experiences of the legal proceedings were over (as we supposed), it was thought best by the women of the Association to make some changes in the usual order of things. After some discussion as to time and place of holding the future meetings of the Association, it was unanimously agreed that this whole subject should be referred to the Executive Committee of ladies and the ministers of the several

Churches; hence a called meeting for the purpose was appointed.

During the next week this meeting was held, and the following plans agreed upon: First, the morning meetings were dispensed with for one week, as an experiment, the afternoon meetings and the visitations substituting them. Evening union temperance services in the Presbyterian church on Monday, in the Baptist church on Tuesday, and in the Methodist Episcopal church on Thursday evening of each week were decided upon. All-day prayer-meetings were held in the churches occasionally. These services proved to be of great interest and profit to the many who attended them. Testimonies full of vital importance were given by not only workers at these meetings, but by many men as well as women, who had been spiritually benefited by this " Temperance Pentecost."

A very great effort was made by a committee, appointed for the purpose, to secure good and reliable speakers for our evening meetings. Several invitations were sent abroad to earnest workers in the State, such as Mrs. Wells, Dr. Staunton, and others; but so great was the demand upon them that we were disappointed. Then we turned to some among ourselves, whose constant occupation in the field of labor assigned them by Providence had prevented their joining

in the daily round of Crusade services for which
they felt the most earnest sympathy: pre-eminently among these was Miss Emily Grand
Gerard, a native French lady, but one who had
been educated by our own Dr. Mathews and was
in full and hearty accord with "every good word
and work." She was principal of the Presbyterian Institute for Young Ladies, and her friends
were legion in all Churches and circles, yet her
modesty was only equaled by her ability. She
accepted an invitation to address an evening
union temperance service in the Presbyterian
church, and chose as her subject "The Crusader." After delineating the Crusaders of
olden times in a most attractive manner, she
brought to bear the glorious privilege of the
modern Crusader in such bold relief that all felt
the power of her words, and gave hearty assent
as she exclaimed: "Nor do they throw themselves in the breach unguarded and unarmed.
No valiant Crusader ever went forth to battle
clad in such a panoply as they wear. Our modern Crusader—for we accept the name given in
derision, and will make it as significant of good
as other titles bestowed in the same spirit, Methodist, Huguenot, etc.—is furnished with weapons
from the armory of heaven (Ephesians vi, 10, 11);
and with such equipments who would dare be
discouraged !"

The entire address of this gifted Christian lady was a benediction to the faithful band of workers, and from that evening they assumed the appellation of "Crusaders," counting it a high privilege to suffer persecution in a cause so glorious.

" Remember Lot's wife " is also one of Hillsboro's mottoes, and the weekly meeting all the way along since 1873, held by the temperance women, proves that the live coal of the Crusade is still burning upon the altar.

About the 20th of March, 1874, the members of our Association, realizing the near approach of house-cleaning and other busy days for housekeepers, determined to call a meeting of the Executive Committee for consultation, and on April 23d the following ladies met in the home of Mrs. John A. Smith: Mrs. McDowell, Mrs. Scott, Mrs. J. A. Smith, Mrs. Glascock, Mrs. R. S. Evans, Mrs. Cowden, Mrs. Foraker, Mrs. D. K. Fenner, and Mrs. Thompson. The consultation resulted in returning to the morning meetings and other work. The entire number of members who were in the spirit of "willing workers," were to be divided into four equal parts, to be known as bands A, B, C, and D, each band to have a leader and assistant leader, to be elected monthly. These leaders and assistants were also to be members of the Executive

Committee. Thus, while some were at work in their respective homes, the visitations upon the few remaining open saloons and bars were prayerfully looked after. Grand evening meetings were held in the different churches, and the interest seemed unabated.

X.

WHEN the 7th of February—the day, by previous appointment, for the "all-day mass-meeting"—came around, a heavy snow covered the ground, and still descended in noiseless flakes of purity and beauty. About nine o'clock A. M. the friends from various parts of the county could be seen, all covered white as the cause they represented, making their way to the old Presbyterian Church, where our Committee of Reception, and also a committee of the men *on horses*, met them; the former conducted the visitors into the morning meeting, and the latter the horses and sleighs to the comfortable quarters provided. A little later the New Vienna delegation came in a huge sled, all seated, robed, and drawn by horses, such as only the humane Friends indulge in.

When those dear, brave, good women, with their Friendly bonnets and modest mien, came

walking into that consecrated church with their
minister, Rev. D. Hill, and their conquered foe,
Van Pelt, the whole audience with one accord
arose and joined heartily in singing, "Praise
God, from whom all blessings flow!" A most
inspiring service followed, of song, prayer, and
testimony, until the hour for lunch—hot coffee,
and plenty of everything good—thanks to the
efficient committee of ladies, whose names I find
recorded in the minutes as follows: Mesdames
M. T. Nelson, Judge Evans, J. M. Boyd, John
Jolly, Judge Mathews, James Patterson, Thomas
Miller, Miss Maria Stewart, Miss Lizzie Kerby,
Miss Rachel Counard.

At half-past one o'clock the procession formed
and marched to Music Hall, the women two and
two, the men following. The order of the procession was for the Hillsboro workers, each one
to choose, as far as possible, a visitor as marching companion. The entire picture was impos-
ing, and awed the most rebellious and critical
into silence that was almost oppressive, as we
marched quietly through a phalanx of wonder-
ing eyes.

The meeting at the hall was a rare one.
Fine music from the soul, an earnest, sensible
address by Rev. D. Hill, followed by the famous
ex-saloon keeper, Van Pelt, who, in a humble,
feeling manner, to all human appearances, gave

reason for faith in his changed condition. His contrition seemed heartfelt, and his alleged allegiance to the cause he had so grossly persecuted, hearty and real. After his talk, there was much feeling, and some one started that blessed hymn,

> "Jesus paid it all,
> All the debt I owe."

Then General McDowell, our right-hand champion on all occasions of a public nature, spoke most effectively, and was followed by Dr. P. H. Wever, whose mind seemed to take in the far-reaching results of Van Pelt's surrender, and in facts and figures demonstrated it in a clear and impressive manner. The audience was then dismissed, and, after hand-shakings and benediction, all returned to their homes, strong in the faith of final victory.

In view of the injunction of Mr. Dunn, it was decided by our Association that we would go on with our temperance work in the churches, halls, and visitations, in our charity work, children's meetings, distribution of temperance literature, canvassing for signatures to the total abstinence pledge, etc., just as we had been doing, save that Mr. Dunn should be left undisturbed with his lawyers until after court. In the meantime our "counsel" had been secured, and we felt at ease, having "done what we could," and

resting upon the assurance "if God be for us,
who can be against us?" No malice or ill-will
was indulged in on the part of temperance
women, as the following resolutions, adopted at
an evening meeting, February 20th, testify:

" WHEREAS, We, the women of the Hillsboro Temperance Association, are greatly encouraged in our
work, God having graciously manifested that he is still
leading us on,—

" *Resolved*, That, while as a body we continue our
work with renewed vigor, strong in faith, the principle
of love and charity shall ever govern us.

" *Resolved*, That while our hearts overflow with gratitude to God that we may be instruments in his hands,
we, as an Association utterly discard any expressions
of triumph and exultation, and will at any time stead-
fastly rebuke any spirit of ridicule or unkindness which
may be manifested at any of our meetings."

These resolutions were offered by Mrs. W.
Doggett, one of our lovely spirits now in heaven,
and were heartily indorsed by the entire Society.
Mrs. Thompson, as recorded in the minutes,
then offered the following resolution, which, after
the lapse of nearly twenty years, she reindorses:

" *Resolved*, That we ladies here present express our
thanks for the wise and prudent counsels of the gentlemen, and their generous conduct towards us in our temperance work."

Persistent, earnest effort had been going on in
the way of visitations, prayer, song, and persua-

sions, in connection with the three remaining
saloons—Ward, Bales, and Uhrig. To all human
appearances these men seemed "joined to their
idols," and yet we did not feel at liberty to "let
them alone." So one icy morning a service was
held on the pavement in front of the Uhrig saloon.
Some of the good, thoughtful ladies of the neighborhood sent door-rugs for the comfort of the
women in kneeling, and Mrs. Foraker, mother
of Ex-Governor Foraker, who was called upon
to lead in the first prayer that morning, took one
of these little rugs, and, placing it upon the top
step, kneeled upon it, and with her mouth at the
key-hole, proceeded to offer one of her apostolic
prayers. When she finished that prayer, and
descended the steps to join her sisters in song
on the pavement, some one asked her, in an
undertone, why she did it, and added: "It
looked so queer."

Her answer was: "When a man locks his
door on good women's prayers, he is apt to be
listening inside to hear what they have to say
about it." And sure enough that prayer was
heard. The young man inside was not destitute
of that tenderness of conscience begotten by
early religious teachings. He had two uncles,
ministers in Fatherland, but love of money "made
easy," and the "national toleration" for what
God has pronounced "accursed," caused him to

see no harm in it; *so he sold.* But he was miserable because of the women's prayers, songs, and entreaties, and he decided to close his establishment, and seek a better way.

There was a feeling of real interest in disposing of the liquors of his saloon, so that no one should be harmed by them; therefore we entered into a business contract, each choosing a "daysman" to settle prices, and so on. The ladies of the committee determined that the liquor owned by Mr. Uhrig should be bought and burned, as none of our Society wished to injure the young man's worldly prospects; his store also underwent a process of invoicing, and upon a fixed day the ladies met, and purchased all there was for sale. As I was a little late, I found no choice in the trophies; but spying a handsome Cognac bottle, I found that it belonged to the partner's wife. In his boyhood days he had been our little neighbor, so I said: "Henry, won't you ask her to sell it to me?" He returned from her room quickly with her consent, and the price affixed; to-day that Cognac bottle, so delicately painted, has a place of honor, as a relic of the "Hillsboro Crusade," in the castle of Lady Henry Somerset, in England.

8

XI.

THE *Highland News*, one of the leading journals of our town, edited by Mr. J. L. Boardman, a champion for temperance and a loyal friend of the woman's movement, on March 10, 1873, had the following:

"The record of the day is not complete without some mention of the outdoor mass-meeting, held on the public square about four o'clock in the afternoon.

"Mr. Uhrig having yielded to the entreaties of the ladies, closed his saloon, and surrendered his liquors. It was determined that the whisky should be burned. A large concourse of people assembled to witness the ceremony.

"The ladies of the Association came in procession from the church, and formed a circle around the three barrels, being marshaled by Mr. Jacob Sayler, who, at their request, had charge of the proceedings.

"After a prayer by Rev. S. D. Clayton, the heads of the barrels were broken in, and the liquor set on fire. The scene was one of solemn joy, never to be forgotten by those who participated in it.

"As the words of prayer were borne heavenward on the wings of the evening air, tears of thankfulness flowed from many eyes, and in the hush which followed the fervent 'Amen,' voices, all tremulous with emotion, joined in the grand old 'John Brown' chorus.

"Even the boys forgot their usual shout and whistle, and the dear familiar hymns, that have cheered and helped us all along the weary way, seemed the fittest expression of our joy. When all was over, the ladies and gentlemen of the Association returned to the church to unite in a song and prayer of solemn thanksgiving to God, being more than ever convinced that he who began the work has continued it, and will in his own good time and way complete it.

" MRS. DEAN K. FENNER, *Secretary.*"

About the beginning of April, 1874, the morning meetings were resumed, and, by special invitation from the " powers that be," they were held alternate weeks in the Presbyterian and Methodist Churches. It must not be forgotten that, in addition to the injunction case, which had been tried at the February term of court, Mr. Dunn had also brought suit against the Crusaders for alleged trespass, and asked *ten thousand dollars damages.* This suit was not to come on for some months, owing to the fact that the parties were not ready for trial. Meantime, the women decided not to "trespass" upon the Palace Drugstore, as there was plenty to do in other directions, and they had no desire, even in appearance, to defy the law. But from an article taken from the *Highland News* about that time, it would seem that our temperance gentlemen were not so minded; for they were busy in the line of legal suasion. In order to give the situation, as its was regarded in this region in 1874, this clipping will be useful

"MR. DUNN IN TROUBLE AGAIN—HE IS BOUND OVER ON
   EIGHT ADDITIONAL CHARGES OF ILLEGAL LIQUOR-
   SELLING.

"Since our last issue, the temperance men have been making things rather uncomfortable for Mr. Dunn, of injunction notoriety, and have pretty effectually stripped him of the borrowed plumage he has hitherto been allowed to wear as a seller of liquor only in strict accordance with the law. He has been arrested, and bound over to court on *eight* distinct charges of illegal selling.

"All these cases but two are for selling liquor to be drank on the premises, and the proof against him is clear in every case. The other two cases are for selling liquor to minors, and in these also the evidence is strong and direct.

"This is all there is in the cry of '*persecution,*' which is being raised by his friends and sympathizers."

The only remaining saloons were the two we first visited, kept by John Bales and Robert Ward, and they were still visited with songs, prayers, and earnest entreaties, until it really seemed a question as to how long they could resist, and how long the Crusaders could patiently endure.

These men were very different in their temperaments. Bales had one song, which he never failed to sing: "Just as soon as the druggists all sign the pledge, and quit selling contrary to law,

then I will quit, and join in with the temperance
people, heart and soul."

Poor Ward always agreed that liquor-selling
was a "bad business," and protested that when-
ever he could sell his house, he would "quit the
business entirely." But when one of our wealthy
citizens (to gratify his noble Crusade wife) offered
him his price for the property, *cash down*, with
a view, we have always believed, of handing it
over to her for Crusade headquarters, the in-
fatuated Ephraim proved his devotion to his idol
by asking five hundred dollars more for his house.
Thus the sale was lost.

Quite a new line of activity opened up about
this time for temperance workers. The Consti-
tutional Convention had at last finished its labors,
and Ohio was required to consider the new constitution. In consequence of the great pressure
brought upon the members of this Convention
by the temperance movement, they saw plainly
that, in order to meet the question fairly, they
would have to submit to the people a choice as
to which of two clauses should be inserted in the
constitution—one favoring the system of license
to sell intoxicating liquors, the other opposed to
license. 'T is true the women had no vote on
the subject, but they would be the greatest suf-
ferers should the State license this terrible traffic.
So when meetings were appointed throughout

the county in school-houses and churches, the
Crusaders accepted the many calls that were
made upon them, and in little groups of three,
four, or six, sought quietly the rural gatherings,
where, from full hearts (and many times bitter
experiences), they reasoned with their neighbors
of "righteousness, temperance, and judgment to
come," and, from the kindly letters received and
published, one might well suppose the novel
work of the women during those days of toil
and danger, was not in vain. As a tribute to
the author of the following letter, we feel that it
should be published in our "Crusade Sketches."
In his little town, Belfast, Highland County,
Mr. Isaac Hottinger, a sensible farmer, had stood
like a granite statue against taunts, ridicule, and
sarcasm, voting the only Prohibition ticket for
so many years, that he naturally hailed the new
movement with enthusiasm:

BELFAST, March 21, 1874.

EDITOR NEWS,—To-day, after religious service was
ended in the Methodist Episcopal Church, Isaac Hottinger moved that we extend our hearty congratulations
and sympathies to the noble women of Hillsboro for their
zealous labors to supress intemperance. Rev. Mr. Am-
brose called for a vote of the House, and I believe it was
carried unanimously, and Isaac Hottinger was appointed
a committee to report the same to the women of Hillsboro, through the columns of the *News*.

So far as I have heard our people express their minds,

they are on the side of the women in this temperance movement. It is the foundation principle of this Government that a majority shall rule. Now, if we were to ask every voter in our nation, "Are you in favor of the sale and use of liquor for a beverage?" two-thirds would say, *No.* Then, why are things in such a deplorable condition? The answer is obvious. We are too busy trying to make money, and more anxious for political party victories, than we are for the cause of temperance.

There is one thing certain to my mind: If the *women* had a vote, they would "right-about-face" the liquor-business in short meter.

God grant that the temperance-ball that was started in Hillsboro may roll on, until it shall break down the reign of King Alcohol, and bind him in chains so strong that he will never again be set free to ravage and destroy our homes!   Yours, for temperance,

ISAAC HOTTINGER.

XII.

AN evening service of much interest was held in the Methodist church about the 20th of April. The Rev. S. D. Clayton was called upon for a speech. He responded in an earnest, rousing address, taking for a text the reply of a saloon-keeper in a town near by, when a broken-hearted mother besought him to sell no more liquor to her only son. Said he: "Madam, your son has as good a right to fill a drunkard's grave as any other mother's son, and I will sell to him as long as he has money to pay for it." I only wish a reporter had been on hand, that the words of power and pathos on that occasion could have been preserved; but they were not lost.

From the *News* of May 13, 1874, we clip the following notice:

"Last Saturday, while the ladies of the Temperance League were holding their usual religious exercises in front of Bales's saloon, he got angry, and seizing Mrs. Pickering and Mrs. Shinn by the shoulder, pushed them roughly off the sidewalk. Mrs. Pickering had him arrested for assault, and taken before 'Squire Stoddard, who, after a full hearing, held him to bail in the sum of one hundred dollars."

This notice records the first act of "self-defense" undertaken by our Crusaders; for their uniform *creed* and *practice* had been kindness, prayer, and Christian effort; and while the incident was greatly deplored by the leaders of the "band," yet the kindly and most efficient legal efforts of our friend, the youthful county attorney, Mr. Dumenil, gave such satisfactory results that we, as Crusaders, felt *compensated* in the *evident* sympathy created for the humane side of the question by his noble efforts. Mr. Dumenil has since pleaded for "the right" in a wider field in his Kansas home, where his merits soon

procured for him position and power to make
his principles felt.

At a morning meeting in the old Crusade
Church, about the 25th of May, 1874, a message
came telling of the arrest of Cincinnati's Crusaders, and a city missionary who had for a long
time been preaching on the streets of the city
unmolested.

After prayer was offered in behalf of the persecuted ones, the president was requested to
write to her friends, Mesdames William I. Fee
and S. K. Leavitt, expressive of the heartfelt
sympathy of our entire Association in this their
time of trial. The meeting for the next morning was to be appropriated to prayer and sup-
plication for their particular cases. Before our
meeting adjourned, Mr. Sayler came in with the
cheering news that the Rocky Fork Distillery
was about to close for want of customers, and
that the Lynchburg Distillery was closed. These
being two of Highland County's "high towers
of iniquity," much joy was felt upon the report,
and the grand old doxology was sung "with the
spirit and the understanding," and we were dismissed by Brother McSurely with a tender benediction in reference to the treatment of Cincinnati's noble women.

Some time before a committee had been
empowered to name a number of gentlemen

who would serve in a county and township temperance organization. The following gentlemen agreed, and a more judicious selection could not have been made: General McDowell, Judge Mathews, Drs. P. H. Wever, H. S. Fullerton, and Marshall A. Nelson. The accepted mission was at once entered upon by this committee, and the Crusaders responded very heartily to all invitations to aid in this work of the new temperance organization.

XIII.

IN view of the increasing business that seemed to be opening up before our Association, a meeting of the Executive Committee was called, and the appointment of two vice-presidents resulted—Mrs. John A. Smith and Mrs. Judge Evans—and our women felt greatly strengthened by the addition of two such aids for future conflicts.

When we assembled the following morning for the appointed prayer service in behalf of our brave but persecuted Cincinnati sisters, it so turned out that the Pittsburg Crusaders were in like peril, and although their names were then less familiar than since, sympathy in the same glorious cause made us one in the Master.

Further reports gave the assurance that these noble women were persecuted even more cruelly than Cincinnati's martyrs! And so our tears and our songs, our prayers and our rejoicings in being among those who were counted worthy to suffer persecution for Christ's sake, caused us to sit together in a heavenly place that morning.

Much enthusiasm was felt and expressed by ministers and laymen. Dr. McSurely on that morning expressed his opinion as to the political drift of the movement. He seemed to believe that "the contest would finally be between American ideas of liberty and right, and the German infidel idea of uncontrolled license, not only in regard to temperance but to all the principles of truth for which our Puritan ancestry braved the terrors of-the New England wilderness, and which they sealed and established with their blood!"

After a lapse of nearly twenty years, these words of our faithful Crusade friend and brother seem prophetic, as we scan the existing struggle (political) between right and wrong, and witness the "Sunday-closing" experience of American statesmen against the uncontrolled and "infidel" ideas of foreign powers, the worst element of which has the privilege of the ballot on American soil. It is well that the women still "cling

to the promises and look up," as the old colored
Baptist brother said he did when he fell; for our
God's promise is sure and steadfast. " The way
of the wicked he turneth upside down;" and
"though it tarry, wait for it, because it will
surely come."

There was much accomplished during the
weeks following,—boxes packed and sent to
flood-sufferers; meetings for the young people
and the children; visitations to the prison by
our faithful committee, Miss Julia Brown, Mrs.
Stevenson, Mrs. Pickering, and others. But,
above all, the county meetings at church and
school-house were vigorously sustained.

About the 23d of June it was suggested and
approved, at the morning meeting, that arrangements be made for having a grand temperance
picnic at the fair-ground on the Fourth of July,
and that a notice and general invitation be published in the town papers and by posters, so that
all good friends of the cause throughout the
county might have ample time to make their
plans to join us. After much labor and great
executive ability on the part of the officers in
charge, committees were decided upon as follows: Arrangement, speakers, music, program,
reception of delegates from townships, marshal
of the day, chairman, secretary, and reporter.

The day's success proved to many a doubter

the coming, quiet, orderly beauty in store for humanity, when "righteousness shall cover the earth" and "the beauty of the Lord our God be upon us." There was fine music (gratis) from the Hillsboro orchestra, and good speaking. Large, spreading oaks shaded the beautiful green sward below, on which each township delegation was received by a committee of Hillsboro Crusaders, and welcomed under their own marked bower. Many smiling visitors from the town, also, who had failed to join in the saloon feature of our work, were free to appreciate and commend the "lovely effects of the Crusade in the Fourth of July celebration," especially when they saw the honest joy it gave the Crusading ladies to provide the best they had for the refreshment of the wives and children of the ex-saloon-keepers.

The first business of note after the successful "Fourth" was the resignation of our valued recording secretary, Mrs. D. K. Fenner, who had served us so faithfully from the first day of our work, and had kept the record so much in the spirit of our Crusade that no word of bitterness or malice could be found upon the "minutes," although diligent search was made (as confessed by Mr. Dunn's attorneys), hoping thereby to establish the plea of persecution against their client. Mrs. Fenner's needed absence from home

made her resignation a necessity, hence we submitted. But in the good providence of God,
who "sets one thing over against another," we
were greatly rejoiced to find that Miss Virginia
H. Wever was willing to serve us, and her name
being duly presented, she was elected unanimously by a rising vote, and from July 13 to
October 29, 1874, we rejoiced in her prompt,
efficient aid, and in her unusual ability as a
parliamentarian, which at that early date of our
Crusade was rare.

The absorbing theme in hamlet, county, and
town now was the approaching test-vote—license
or no license. To this end Rev. Dr. Leonard,
then of Cincinnati, had been invited to Hillsboro, and on the evening before the election
made one of his masterly efforts in Music Hall,
which had a very fine effect upon the minds of
our people. As usual, the amiable Crusaders
had worked hard all the weeks of the past "no-
license campaign," and now, at the crisis, they
could not use the only effective weapon in such
an emergency; but they felt assured that their
cry would be heard at the court of heaven;
hence, an all-day prayer, song, and conference
meeting was held on the day the men voted.
The burden of the prayers that day was: "O,
Lord, help the men to vote *right* in thy sight,
and hasten the day when the curse of home may

be banished from this and every land!" And all
the Crusaders (women and men) said, *Amen.*

At the evening service, after learning of our
victories, General McDowell, the uniform friend
of the ladies in their efforts in the temperance
work, paid a high tribute to their efficiency in
the late conflict, and said emphatically: "It is
my opinion that the work and speaking of the
women saved the township and county on the
18th." Thereupon the Rev. S. D. Clayton arose
and said: "Yes, General, when I heard of the victory in Liberty Township and Highland County,
I said, and now repeat it, 'May the Lord bless
these earnest, noble women!' and he will."

XIV.

AT the close of the summer of 1873, Auxiliary
Temperance Leagues had been formed in
almost every township of Highland County. The
license clause of the new State Constitution had
been defeated, and, although all had not been accomplished in our own community that was de-
sired or sought after, yet there was a state of
reformation and safety existing that furnished at
least great hopes for the future.

A call came about this time from a duly-au-
thorized group of Christian ladies—women who

had "drawn near to God in saloon prayer-meetings"—and "as they recounted the wonders of the great uprising" at the restful retreat, Chautauqua, their hearts "burning within them" for still greater work, so this call was made upon every League of temperance women in the Crusade States. They were requested to call Cconventions for the purpose of electing a woman from each congressional district as delegate to an organizing Convention, to be held in the city of Cleveland, O., November 18–20, 1874.

The history of that memorable Convention at Cleveland and its origin was so well delineated by the graceful pen of our Crusade sister, Mrs. W. A. Ingham, of Cleveland, for the Louisville Convention of the National W. C. T. U., that I wish every White-ribbon sister had a copy of it in her own scrapbook. We poor mortals fail, ofttimes, to take in the meaning of events as they pass, but afterward the handwriting of divinity becomes legible. Surely it was so with some of us in the case of that first National Temperance Convention of women.

It was my high privilege to have received the majority vote from our district as the delegate to that Convention; and but for the fact that our beloved State president, Mrs. Prof. McCabe, of Delaware, Ohio, would be there, and with her gentle, sweet, cultured womanhood afford an apology for

such a venture, I should hardly have felt that I
could accept; for Conventions had always been
associated in my mind with men of business, of
Church or State, and especially with political
nominations. True, I had been led by the Spirit
and the convulsion of events to pray in saloons
and on the street; but what would we gain by
bearing the persecutions resulting from holding
Conventions? After the lapse of twenty years,
let the organized power of woman in the temperance reform of the world answer this question!

The minutes of our Association, so accurately
and beautifully kept by our secretary, Miss Wever,
during these days and weeks of uneventful toil,
show much of interest, but of such a purely local character that we must not overburden our
pages. The morning prayer-meetings, evening
mass-meetings, three times each week in the different churches, the children's gatherings once a
week, and the young people's three times each
month, with much interest in connection with
many other avenues of usefulness, continued until
January 1, 1874, when the ministers expressed a
desire to hold religious services each in their own
churches, hoping thereby to conserve the spiritual developments of the Crusade in a more personal and pronounced way than could be done in
the general temperance-meetings. They can not
be accused of a sectarian spirit in this; for in the

9

language of one of their number, our faithful Crusade Brother Cowden, of the Methodist Episcopal Church, they all agreed. He said at an evening meeting just before the program was changed: "I shall not be here many weeks longer; but no matter where I shall go in the providence of God, or how long I shall live, we can never forget the pleasant hours spent in Hillsboro, and particularly the pleasantness of the temperance work—where Christians forgot their denominational lines and escaped from their sectarian prejudices, to labor as one Church, as one family in Christ, for the great cause of temperance! I confess the closer I am brought into relationship with our Churches, and the more I know about them, the more I love them."

When the time came around for the observance of our Crusade anniversary, December 23, 1874, there was but one feeling. Our grand army of pledged children being, as the Crusaders felt, their brightest trophies of the year's work, it was determined to make it a children's passover; and most happy was the thought, for at two o'clock in the afternoon on the 23d, parents and children, Crusaders and ministers, all combined to raise a grateful Ebenezer in the old church, where, one year before, a few women had timidly sung, "Give to the winds thy fears!"

A meeting of the temperance women was

called for March 8, 1875, at the Methodist Episcopal church.   A letter was read from   Mrs.
William I. Fee, of Cincinnati, urging the ladies
of Hillsboro to give their aid in getting up the
State Temperance Fair, to be held in Cincinnati
the second week of April.   The Crusaders, old
and young, entered into the scheme with zeal.
A Committee of Arrangements was formed of
the following ladies, who were to meet for further
consultation at Mrs. Thompson's on the next
day: Mesdames Rev. Weatherby, James Patterson, D. K. Fenner, Miss Virginia H. Wever, Miss
Ella Dill.   Very soon a beautiful contribution of
fancy and useful articles was ready, and, at the
time appointed, the ladies elected to sustain the
Hillsboro table at the fair were off for the scene
of action.   A beautiful canopy of drab material,
ornamented with golden letters, shaded with
black and red, handsomely formed, gave forth
from the old Hillsboro table this sentiment:

"DEATH TO THE TRAFFIC,

BUT

LIFE TO THE SLAVE."

Much kindly feeling was the result of this united
effort, and some money in the temperance treasury of the State for future work.

XV.

THE DUNN TRIAL.

ON the 30th day of January, 1874, a suit for
$10,000 damage was brought by David
Johnson and Wm. H. H. Dunn, druggists of
Hillsboro, Ohio, against the temperance people
engaged in the work of reform, known as the
"Woman's Crusade." This suit was called an
"action of trespass," and was tried at the May
term of the Court of Common Pleas, in the year
1875, before the Hon. T. M. Gray, R. T. Hough
being clerk of said court, and Cary T. Pope,
sheriff. Counsel for the plaintiff were Sloan &
Smith, Collins & Dittey, Henry L. Dickey, and
Judge Safford. Counsel for the defendants,
A. F. Perry, Cincinnati; M. J. Williams, Toledo;
James H. Thompson, A. G. Matthews, and
George B. Gardener, of Hillsboro.

The eventful morning, 17th of May, 1875,
when "the ladies" were requested to take their
seats in the court-room, came at last. There
was much curiosity as to the conduct of the
Crusaders; but the slow, solemn peal of the
old church-bell at eight o'clock satisfied all that
they had not forgotten their morning prayer-
meeting. Every woman was at her post promptly
on *that morning*, and our bright, brave young

ladies, who were so true and useful during those
Crusade days of self-denial and cross-bearing,
were on hand in full force, and never did their
sweet, clear voices ring out with such pathos as
on that occasion.

Precious promises from God's own Word were
read by the leader. "My faith looks up to Thee,"
was sung with much feeling; then a few brief,
earnest prayers were offered, just to the point,
notably Mrs. Foraker's, which made a lasting
impression upon all hearts. She appealed to
the Lord, "in his righteousness, to confuse and
confound the lawyers who were engaged in prose-
cuting the women of Hillsboro (who were his
believing children) for trying to remove the
stumbling-blocks out of the way of the weak,
and to establish his righteous laws for the protection of the sons and daughters of our community."

After joining with "one heart and one mind"
in the amen to that prayer, the doxology was
sung; then, two-and-two, the line of march was
taken up, with modest mien but brave hearts,
for the *court of justice.*

The Crusaders were conducted to the seats
assigned them, and, after quietly taking in the
situation, the first thing that attracted attention
was the heaps of law-books profusely marked,
that were piled upon the table by which sat

Judge Safford (senior attorney for Dunn). Naturally, we " poor, weak women felt, Can there be
so much against us in those books of doom?
But we cried still more earnestly (in our hearts),
"O Lord, undertake for us !"

For some time after we took our seats the
judge seemed very much absorbed examining
these books, and marking new points of law;
finally he took his glasses off, placed them in a
bright morocco case, laid them down on the
table (unfortunately too near the edge), and,
gracefully turning himself, so as to give attention to the speaker, who was very earnestly
" opening the case," lost sight of his spectacles.
Quick as thought, our officious little dog (named
" Busy Bee " by his little master, because of his
perpetual motion), danced up on his hind legs to
the table, where he spied the bright spectacle-
case, and, taking the tip-end between his little
white teeth, darted off under tables and seats
to—nobody knew where. Very soon there was
occasion for some of those marked portions
of legal lore, and the spectacles were in demand, but search was made in vain. The "con-
fusion " that followed was "confounding." No
one, save myself, seemed to know of the dog's
trick, and I was called out to meet an expected
guest; but as I was passing hastily out, Mrs.
Foraker drew me down to her, and, with her

expressive face all aglow, said: "I do believe I prayed a little too hard."

The court-room was crowded every day by visitors from town and vicinity, and from a distance. In the hope of convicting the Crusaders of damaging Mr. Dunn's trade, many witnesses had been subpœnaed. Examinations and cross-examinations were indulged in on both sides, to the utter weariness of all concerned. Finally the argument, in all its variety commenced, and, as the minutes have it, "arguments, reason, logic, pathos, humor, impassioned defense, and malicious personalities, which are better forgotten than recorded;" after which the judge charged the jury. The eagerness with which its action was awaited can well be imagined. The countenances of the Crusaders said in legible lines of unrest, "Vain is the help of man," remembering the rulings of the judge; but when the bell rang, hundreds from the outside, willing to shout for the winning side, flocked to the court-house to hear the doom. The jury, obliged to base their decision upon the legal proofs in the case, as allowed by the court, found the defendants guilty of trespass. And as it was proved that Mr. Dunn lost the sale of a gallon of coal-oil and some other trifling matter in consequence of the presence of the ladies on his steps and sidewalks, the damages were put at

five dollars instead of ten thousand; but that
was enough to throw the costs upon the temperance men.   Immediately a bill of exceptions
was made to Judge Gray's rulings by counsel for
the defense, and the case was sent to the Superior
Court.   Expectation was quite general that the
decision would be reversed; but it never was, because the active member of the firm, Wm. H. H.
Dunn, soon after took the benefit of the bank-
rupt law, and his assignee declined to defend the
suit in the Supreme Court.   The costs were settled, and the wrath of man became as "stubble
fully dry," and was "devoured," as was promised
in Nahum i, 10.

XVI.

AFTER the weariness and excitement of the
Dunn trial, the undaunted, invincible Crusaders met again in the dear old church where
their first vows were recorded, and proceeded to
business as quietly and peacefully as though they
had not been under the arrest of human judgment, feeling in their hearts the comforting assurance, "If God be for us, who can be against
us?"   The devotions on that day were solemn
and impressive, and plans for future work were
entered into with harmony and zeal.

First, it was decided to meet weekly, at the

homes of the members of the League alternately, for prayer and conference; once each month a public temperance-meeting should be held in one of the churches; children's temperance-meeting once a week, and the young people of the town be urged to continue their gatherings three times each month. The feeling had been growing on the part of the ladies that a room set apart for their own line of work was a necessity, and they voted unanimously in favor of immediate action. Later, by appointment, the following committee took charge of the matter: Mesdames Dr. Sams, D. K. Fenner, S. Janes, J. Stevenson, E. J. Thompson. From the minutes we find: "Monday evening, December 6, 1875, the general monthly temperance-meeting was held in the League-room for the first time. By the united request of the ladies, Dr. McSurely conducted the services of dedicating our little temple to God and humanity, and it was done in a manner most helpful and pleasing to all in attendance. After singing 'He leadeth me,' Mrs. Thompson was asked to give the history of the League-room, how it was obtained, how and by whom furnished, etc. This she did, and demonstrated fully that the whole thing was a *special providence*."

The detailed account as given then would be uninteresting at this late day; but we may, with righteous pride, turn to our "temple" in Chicago, the outcome of "woman's faith."

This humble old building was divided by a slight partition into two rooms. Removing this line of separation, we had a respectable oblong room, with front door and two windows, the same in the rear. Plaster, paint, paper, scrubbing-brushes, carpet, seats, tables, stove, blinds, mottoes, pictures, Bible, and books of song and many other conveniences, were all the spontaneous offerings of earnest hearts. Not one dollar of debt was left upon the ladies when the first songs of praise and voice of prayer were heard under that lowly, consecrated roof.

A series of morning meetings of a devotional character had been arranged to follow the opening service of the League-room. These meetings were to be presided over by the Crusaders, alternately, and this Tuesday morning service was assigned to me. As our audience increased, and the sweet songs of Zion floated out upon the clear, crisp air of that December morning, a noble heart for whom earnest prayers were ascending from that sacred place felt "strangely drawn;" and when the dignified form of General McDowell entered this newly-dedicated "temple," and took a seat near the door, there was a visible mark of answered prayer upon the faces of many present.

After several prayers, songs, and telling experiences, the leader invited her "Uncle Mc-Dowell" (in a friendly way) to say something to them; as he had throughout the Crusade been such a wonderful stay and help to the ladies, all felt a desire to hear from him now in their new line of work. At once he arose, laid off his overcoat, and, walking slowly up towards the front said, with quivering lip: "I am not worthy to speak before you good women. During the war I grew more and more hardened and embittered, as those professing Christianity vilified each other, and brothers shed their own brother's blood. I confess I came to believe there was no such thing as religion. But I have watched the Crusaders with an interest few understood, and as I have seen those among you who were tenderly reared, kneel upon the sawdust floors—yea, even upon the pavements in front of barred doors—and have heard them, with tears coursing down their cheeks, pray for their worse than murderers, and for their wives and children, and then have followed them to the churches, and found the same spirit evinced there, I have been led to feel—yes, *that is the Christ love!* And I want to tell you, my dear sisters, that I feel it in my heart this morning!" He was deeply moved, and so were all who heard him. And that dear little wife, our first vice-president and zealous Crusader, who

had prayed so faithfully for the beloved husband
of her youth for fifty years, now realized with
new joy the faithfulness of her covenant-keeping
God, and joined the happy group of sympathiz-
ing friends in songs of praise. That meeting,
long to be remembered, closed with a new seal
of God's approval upon the Crusade, and a
recognition of his presence in our "gospel temperance" meetings.

General McDowell lost no time in communi-
cating with his friend and pastor, Dr. McSurely,
and at once renewed his early membership with
the Presbyterian Church. From the hour of his
new life-experience his growth in grace, and
marvelous Christian development were "known
and read of all men;" for the tender Savior knew
how soon he would be called from labor to reward; hence he made of him a "shining light."
General Joseph J. McDowell was a successful
man in life, possessed a fine personal appearance,
was an attractive speaker, fine conversationalist,
and during his terms of public service in State
and National Councils, won laurels, socially as
well as politically. But what were all these
perishable gifts and graces to that touch of
"Divine love" which transformed his nature
into the "image of the heavenly," and made him
meet for the kingdom that "endureth forever?"

XVII.

THE result of the Spirit's influence in the meetings at the League room was most manifest and helpful, and yet the loss of the sweet songs of Zion on the early morning air in our Crusade services seemed greatly missed by many; indeed it had been to the outside world as an open-air concert, because of the superior voices of our faithful and devoted leaders, the three sisters, Annie, Bessie, and Maggie Wilson. The two elder especially were our reliance—for they allowed none of their active home duties (never neglected) to hinder prompt attention to the song-service of church, street, or saloon; their bright faces and the clear, soft melody of their voices gave inspiration to many a faint heart during those days of early rising, hard work, and bitter persecution. Aided by the many young ladies of our town who possessed gifts of voice, spirit, and will, the Crusade movement was peculiarly fortunate in this department.

But now that we must needs be shut up, as it were, in close communion, under our own vine and fig-tree, as compensation for the loss of much that was inspiring we almost daily witnessed God's power in some new and striking demonstration of the Spirit. Reports were now brought

into our League-room meetings of conversions in
prison through our zealous sisters in charge of
that work, and letters were read from prisoners
in our county jail who felt they were God's free
men, saved from their sins by the merits of
Christ and the kindness and the prayers of the
good women.   After the release of one of these
men from prison a request was sent to the Society that he might, before leaving for his home,
be permitted to attend one meeting in our blessed
League-room.   Consent was gladly given, and
some of our faithful men were invited to meet
with us.

As the time drew on for our anniversary, the
general feeling was that the day must have special attention, and a meeting was called for ma-
turing plans, in fulfillment of which, on Thursday
evening, December 23, 1875, Mrs. D. K. Fenner,
as secretary of the Woman's League, gave a con-
densed report of the Crusade from the first morning, 1873, until present date, 1875.   Mrs. Pickering, as secretary of the children's work, reported
that branch, and Dr. McSurely (by the earnest
request of the ladies) gave a finished address,
showing that "this movement, extending as it
has in its influence over the whole civilized world,
is an inspiration of God's Holy Spirit."   Thus
was marked the second "milestone" of the
Woman's Crusade in Hillsboro.

At the regular monthly meeting, January 5, 1876, after devotional exercises and reading the minutes, it stands recorded: "Mrs. Thompson proposed that a committee be appointed at once to canvass the town for more subscribers to the woman's paper, *The Union Signal.*"

The next business in order was the consideration of a letter from Mrs. H. C. McCabe, Ohio's president, with regard to a plan of her own devising, whereby the State treasury might be supplied, as at this early stage of our work it was empty.

Each local Union was requested to send to her, at Delaware, a square of silk of given dimensions, patchwork, quilted or embroidered, but lined with linen, the usual gray color, and on that linen lining the names of all members who would send a dime or more must be written legibly, and if possible, in fadeless ink.

Our ladies at once responded, favoring the scheme, and a committee was appointed to take charge of the Hillsboro block for the "Ohio Crusade quilt." Mrs. Weatherby, who was superintendent of the Children's Temperance Band at that time, provided a beautiful square for them, and sent it, with $5, each child giving five cents with the name. Our woman's block was embroidered handsomely, and $10 in dimes sent with it.

During the winter of 1876 the different Churches of our town had been faithfully served by their respective pastors with protracted services, and yet, the "partition walls" having been so effectually removed during the Crusade, there was a great desire, on the part of the Christian women especially, that there should be a union service, where all denominations could once more meet around one common "mercy-seat." The subject was brought up at our meetings in the League room, and finding no opposition, it was made a subject of earnest prayer.

Very soon matters were all adjusted. The Methodist Episcopal church being the largest in town, was, by consent of the pastor, Rev. Lucien Clark, and trustees, agreed upon as the proper place for holding these services. Nathan and Esther Frame had been secured as evangelists, and for weeks a most blessed revival of religion refreshed and strengthened all denominations.

The humble little League room was found quite too small for the new additions to our numbers, who flocked to our gospel temperance-meetings; hence the women of the Union quickly procured and fitted up another hall, with dimensions ample for all purposes, even the children's meetings.

At the regular monthly temperance-meeting, May 1, 1876, it is stated in the minutes that, by request, Mrs. Thompson gave a concise account of the progress of the work during the past two months. She also spoke of the work in Brooklyn, N. Y., and of its wonderful results, expressing her confidence in the ultimate success of the cause. Her address was followed by short speeches from Rev. Mr. Bowen, of the Episcopal church; General McDowell, and Judge Mathews. A letter was read, addressed to Mrs. Thompson, from the national president, Mrs. Wittenmeyer, requesting the Hillsboro Crusaders to send a telegraphic protest to the Centennial Commission against permitting the sale of intoxicating liquors on the Centennial Fair grounds. Such telegram was at once forwarded, and paid for by the League. Mrs. Wittenmeyer also requested the Hillsboro League to contribute to the National Temperance Fair, which was to be held in Philadelphia, beginning the second week in June.

The Crusade fire still burned upon the altar of the Woman's Christian Temperance Union, and it is inspiring at this late date to read in their minutes the comforting facts plainly indicating that the "God of Jacob" was still leading on to the victory, which, unseen by them, was all planned by his mighty love and power.

10

XVIII.

"APRIL 5, 1877—Meeting opened by Mrs. Thompson, who read the 146th Psalm, and suggested that we concentrate our faith and prayers upon the coming of Francis Murphy the following week to our town, that the promises contained in our blessed Crusade psalm may be verified in the hearts and homes of our people, and that the Lord in his mercy may at that time 'raise' some that have been long bowed down." (Minutes.)

The prayers that were then offered came from warm hearts and not from feigned lips! And, as the sequel proved, were heard in heaven, "His dwelling-place," and answered on earth to the joy of many hearts.

The "Murphy Temperance Movement" was inaugurated in Greenfield, Highland County, Ohio, early in the spring of 1877. Hon. Henry L. Dicky, ex-member of Congress of that place, became a convert to the new code of sobriety, "with malice toward none and charity for all," and it had a magical effect upon his brethren of the Hillsboro bar, composed, as it had been for many years, of men possessing unusual talent and rare legal ability, famous, most of them, for social qualities, too often sinfully heightened by that enemy which "steals away the brain." Hence the "Macedonian cry" was the more gladly heeded by the distinguished convert of Greenfield, and he came over to aid our earnest aspirants after a new code of jurisprudence.

On the appointed evening, May 14, 1877, the city hall was lighted up, the Hillsboro orchestra was in fine tune, anxious hearts were throbbing, and all things seemed to take on a readiness for the very remarkable "Temperance Pentecost," which, inaugurated upon that evening, grew to such amazing proportions in our county.

Many of the men who were then redeemed from the curse of appetite are to-day beacon-lights, and some have left

> "Footprints on the sands of time,"

For

> "A forlorn and shipwrecked brother."

The grace of forgiving spirits engendered by the "love that never faileth" was beautifully illustrated in the harmony that characterized the blending of Crusaders and Murphyites in the work which followed; indeed, the prominent counsel on Dunn's side, in his suit against the women of the temperance siege, were for a long time among the most earnest and zealous co-workers in the grand battle for the right in the "Blue Ribbon" army.

For many months the converts to the peaceful, God-trusting card of Francis Murphy formed a self-constituted band of workers, and went into rural districts, and by invitation to adjoining towns, speaking to crowds and gaining signatures to the pledge by the hundreds. And as so many of our "Murphy men" were lawyers, we had the advantage of trained talkers, and much good came of their efforts. Strange to say, when the gospel of temperance takes hold of the conscience, it is apt to inspire the heart with such interest in poor humanity that words are given, as we have seen abundantly proved in this as other communities.

After a visit from Francis Murphy and months of ceaseless labor, the "Murphy men," aided by the Woman's Christian Temperance Union and the ministers of the town, commenced each Sunday afternoon "Murphy meetings" at city hall. These services continued to be well sustained for years, and were always cheered by the faithful few, among them my husband, Judge Thompson, who at this late day is justly proud to be recognized as a successful "Murphy man," and much of the joy of our declining years results from the peaceful blending of the sentiments represented by our badges—white and blue.

During all the years since 1877 the work of

the Crusaders, although taking on new forms of
service and new lines of work, has kept marching on. Notable workers, both women and men,
have from time to time been with us by invitation, and thus we have been greatly strengthened. Since the days of Crusade zeal and
Murphy helpfulness, however, the White-ribbon
sisterhood finds it much more difficult to keep
a full treasury, and many times our aspiration
after the oratory of truth fails to culminate,
simply because we can not afford it, and those
who could help us will not do it.

XIX.

TENTH ANNIVERSARY.

IT was on the morning of December 24, 1873,
that our women first set out, heeding only
the inward voice which said: "This is the way;
walk ye in it." As the tenth anniversary drew
near, the Crusaders were impelled to celebrate it
in a service commensurate with the thanksgiving
in their hearts.

By invitation of the Union, Frances E. Willard, the beloved national president, accompanied by Miss Esther Pugh, treasurer of the
National Woman's Christian Temperance Union,

and Miss Anna Gordon, Miss Willard's faithful
private secretary, came to add honor to the day.
A reception and supper in Music Hall, on the
evening of December 22d, was a financial and
social success. Services for the children were
held on Sunday, 23d, at 2 P. M., conducted by
Miss Gordon in the Presbyterian church, and
assisted by Miss Pugh. A Murphy meeting in
the City Hall, at three o'clock, was in charge of
Rev. Mr. Shade, at which Miss Willard narrated
the call to which she surrendered the cherished
plans of her life to become an evangel to "the
great unwashed, untaught, ungospeled multi-
tude." Exceptionally fine music completed a
memorable service.

A mass-meeting in the evening was presided
over by Mrs. Thompson at the Methodist church,
assisted by Rev. J. W. Weatherby, pastor of the
Baptist Church of Seville, Ohio. Miss Esther
Pugh, with the unflinching principles of her
Friends' faith, and the never-give-up spirit of the
Woman's Christian Temperance Union, was the
most suitable reader of the Crusade psalm. The
battle hymn of the Crusade was most impress-
ively rendered as a quartet and chorus, all of
which made a fine setting for Miss Willard's
thrilling exposition of the results of a decade of
Crusade work. A liberal contribution was made
for the national treasury, and Rev. John Pearson,

presiding elder of the Hillsboro District, invoked the blessing of God at the close.

Storms and cold winds had too long seasoned the spirit of the Crusaders for them to be intimidated by the rigors of the morning of December 24th, which found them assembled in the old Crusade Church with hearts glowing with memory of the goodness of God and the power of the truth. As Miss Mattie Mather said: "The marvelous growth of the Temperance Crusade, now making our quiet conservative town a very Bethlehem, was most aptly illustrated by the ancient legend of the tent in the walnut, brought by an Oriental prince to his father, which being unfolded, covered the king, the councilors, the kingdom and the world."

The same faithful pastor, Dr. McSurely, of this same dear old Church, as true to the cause as ten years before, opened the meeting, but after devotional exercises and cheering comfort of speech, turned the service over to the ladies by calling to the chair the president elected just ten years before. After reading the 146th Psalm, she gave her testimony to the faithfulness of "a covenant-keeping God," who had verified his promises made to her ten years previous, by "vindicating the wrongs of the oppressed," by loosing the prisoners, by opening the eyes of the blind, by raising up those who were bowed down, and by "turning the way of the wicked upside down."

Well knowing that hearts and ears were waiting for the inspired words of Miss Willard, always eloquent and soul-moving, she was doubly so in responding to the invitation to speak on this blessed day.

"Give to the winds thy fears" was sung at her request, after which a memorial paper was read by Mrs. Janes, in which tender record was made of the members of the original Crusade band who had gone from labor to reward, and of whom it might be well said, " Their works do follow them."

TESTIMONIES.

Mrs. General Joseph McDowell gave a brief account of the wonderful conversion of her noble husband at a prayer-meeting in the first room set apart for the use of the temperance women.

Mrs. McDowell gave us many incidents of interest connected with those wonderful days. This stirred the souls of others, and one after another related some striking reminiscence of '73 and '74, until the noon hour admonished us that time was only too short for the pent-up memories of those days of spiritual power.

Mrs. Margaret Stevens, a faithful worker, though a most retiring one, was urged to relate the following incident of the war of bloodless vic-

tories: On one occasion when we were trying to
save the poor men from entering those places of
death, our leader, who was holding a prayer-
meeting in front of a saloon, noticed that the
back entrance was becoming popular, and suggested that it would be well to guard that point.
I said I would be one to go, and Mrs. Doggett
joined me. Very soon two young men approached, evidently not sober. One, having a
gun upon his shoulder, insisted upon having
their rights. We said: "You have no right to
destroy yourselves." The gun was taken down
in a menacing manner by the young man as he
approached me. Just at that instant Mrs. Doggett stepped up, and in her kind, gentle way, laid
her hand upon the shoulder of the young man,
saying: "John, I know how your mother prays for
you, and now we will join her." The gun was
laid down, the tears of contrition began to flow,
and as they left they said: "You are brave, good
Christian women, and we thank you for your interest in us."

Two brave Crusaders from Wilmington, Mrs.
Farquhar and Mrs. Clevenger, had dared the
worst weather that has ever been known in this
region, to come over and help in celebrating our
twenty-third; they gave very earnest words of
sympathy and cheer, and enlivened the meeting
by some of the incidents of their work, which

was so successful that for months they rejoiced in having *no open door* to destruction in their midst.

Two earnest Presbyterian sisters gave wonderful testimony to the power of the Spirit upon their hearts during those days of prayer and sacrifice.

Mrs. Stephenson said the "sword of the Spirit" had severed from her soul (through the influence of the Crusade) that formality of service which for years had enslaved her spirit and fettered her tongue, so as to cause a lifeless, dumb service; that she had been delivered from the fear of the world, and had ever since rejoiced in the will of her Heavenly Father, and continually upon her heart was the psalm of joy, "Praise ye the Lord."

Mrs. Ellifritz gave a most thrilling account of the struggles that she endured with her own spirit when she first went out with the Crusaders—lifetime usages, the rules and forms of her own Church, which in the past, she claimed, had not brought out the latent spiritual power of woman. Finally, after a sore and prolonged battle with the powers of darkness, the Spirit set her free, since which time she had been free indeed.

Mrs. Hart, wife of Mr. Alphonso Hart, who was one of our most earnest and liberal workers, always counting "sacrifice" a portion of "service," gave a talk this morning that appeared to set the

calendar back a decade; for the tongues of fire
that rested upon the original band seemed again
visible. Mrs. D. K. Fenner (first secretary) also
proved the undying nature of this zeal for God
and humanity.

Mrs. Rev. McSurely brought out a very
noticeable feature of our work as Crusaders in
the relation of an incident that occurred just as
we were forming in line for the march to the
street, on our way to do God's work. Some one
said: "Why, Mrs. Thompson, are we really going
to sing and pray in the saloons?" The answer
was: "We don't know what we will do; God
will lead and guide us."

To have heard the experiences of these good
women on this "decennial anniversary" morning
would have proved to the most doubting minds
that the Crusade movement was from God, and
that the purifying and quickening influence of
the Holy Spirit was one of its seals.

Indeed it was a wonderful meeting, one long
to be remembered; and with glad hearts we raised
at this decade our Ebenezer, and sang together
with the sisterhood of all lands, warmed by the
same fire, "Blest be the tie that binds." Again
we set forth with the "sword of the Spirit in
hand," putting on anew the whole armor of God,
resolved to battle with renewed zeal and courage
"for God, and home, and every land."

XX.

THE unexpected changes in the tenor of the Woman's Christian temperance work, at the different eras of the dispensation that came upon them December, 1873, afford proof positive of the divinity of its origin. No finite mind could have inspired the persistence and guided the ever-varied tactics developed in this society of women, young and old, having its origin in the simple faith that God would do for them what they could not do for themselves, if they would obey his voice and walk according to the leadings of his spirit.

When the time came in our town for the Crusaders to decide upon a change of policy regarding their temperance work, special prayer was resorted to, and passages of Scripture, as definitely as the "pillar of fire by night and of cloud by day," directed them. The zeal of the women sought new outlets; speakers of note and influence from abroad were invited, and series of meetings held, causing an increase of interest in the community; and the constancy with which the regular weekly services were persevered in silenced all doubts as to the stability of the cause or the intentions of "these invincible women!"

About the time of "the Week of Prayer," 1888,

it was resolved by the members of the Union to
invite Mrs. Romick, of Ohio, for a week of temperance and gospel work in our town. Measures
were at once set in motion, and on March 20,
1888, she came to us, as our secretary, Mrs. E.
L. Warson, happily expressed it, "with a heart
filled with love for God and humanity, and ready
for work in his cause." The result was, many
were benefited and our Union was built up and
strengthened. Her sweet, humble Christian spirit
will long be remembered among our people.

Mothers' meetings had become a favorite feature of our work, conducted at first by Mrs. E.
J. Patterson, a zealous worker in many depart-
ments, and presided over afterwards by Mrs.
Bridwell.

But, as is always the case, some one person
must be responsible for the outcome of such extra
services, and that person must have a special gift
and preparation. After our dear Mrs. Bridwell
left us for favored Harriman, the mothers' meetings became a thing of the past. But we are
trusting and believing that God will open the
way for its revival.

The 1st of February, 1887, the ministers of
the town, the "Murphy Men," the "Young
Men's League," and other good temperance
voters, circulated a petition asking the Common
Council to provide for a special election, at which

the electors of the city might be granted the privilege of voting for or against the liquor-traffic under the local-option clause of the " Dow Law."

Two hundred signatures of qualified voters were obtained, and the petition was presented on February 7th. The City Council at first refused to grant the petition; but under strong pressure of public sentiment this action was reconsidered, and the election set for March 14, 1887.

At a meeting of the Woman's Christian Temperance Union upon Monday, February 21st, after most earnest devotional exercises, the subject of so much interest took possession of all hearts, and questions of *aid without hindering* caused much anxious discussion. Finally it was proposed that the ladies should furnish a free lunch, to be served in the City Hall, above the voting place on election-day, provided the leading temperance men approved the plan. Another general meeting of the women was appointed to be held in the Methodist Episcopal Church on the following Saturday afternoon, March 5th, and a general invitation issued to the ladies of the county to join them.

The committee in power (of men), through the committee of ladies appointed at a former meeting to confer with them, signified their thanks and hearty approval. At once the women set their hospitable designs to work by the ap-

pointment of five most efficient workers as a
"committee of trust," as to them was assigned
the important obligation of selecting the serving
committee, whose duty it should be to serve the
tables at the hours assigned during the day, from
9 o'clock A. M. to 5 P. M.

A meeting of citizens of all faiths, religious
and political, was called for Saturday evening the
26th, in City Hall, by the ministers of all the
Churches and the signatures of thirty-three
prominent citizens. This meeting was held in
the parlor of the Young Men's League, in the
Methodist Episcopal Church, on the evening of
the 22d; and, by the way, this association of non-
partisan, non-sectarian young men formed a most
hopeful feature of our community. They owed
their origin to the zeal and conservative spirit of
the Rev. Davis W. Clark, son of Bishop Clark
(deceased), and pastor of the Methodist Episcopal
Church of this place at that time. He took a
most active part in this contest, and was urged to
write up the marvelous victory for prohibition in
this Crusade town. From his account of things
we make some quotations for the benefit of those
interested.

Speaking of the meeting that was held on
Saturday, ev ing, February 26th, in City Hall,
he says: "Hon. J. H. Thompson was called to
the chair. To him belongs the honor, not only

of making an admirable opening address, but of having uttered a prophecy of victory, which had literal fulfillment.   Dr. W. J. McSurely, of Crusade fame, followed in a forcible speech."   An Executive Committee was appointed to have charge of the campaign.   Mass-meetings now followed in quick succession, and were sustained by the best talent of this and neighboring communities.

On Tuesday evening, 10th, by invitation of the men's Executive Committee, the Young Men's League held a remarkable meeting in Armory Hall.   Over one hundred young men fell into line, and, with J. M. Hughy for captain, and to the inspiring tap of the drum-corps, they paraded the streets.   This demonstration produced a profound sensation.   It seemed a mute but eloquent appeal.   They were the class most endangered by the existence of the saloon.   When the brave "League boys" filed into the hall and took the seats reserved for them, they received a perfect ovation from the immense audience.

On the Sabbath preceding the election the pulpits rang out with no uncertain sound.   Rev. I. W. Joyce, D. D. (since bishop), arrived from Cincinnati on Saturday evening, by special invitation, and as the *News Herald* has it, " He preached on the subject of temperance at the Methodist Episcopal Church, both morning and

evening, and talked on the same subject at
Armory Hall in the afternoon. He was greeted
with immense and enthusiastic audiences at each
meeting. Rev. Davis W. Clark says:

"Our movement was pre-eminently religious. The
affair had its inception in a meeting of ministers and
under the roof of a church. All public meetings opened
with prayer, and closed with doxology and benediction.
It was a minister's voice in the closing hours of our
struggle that called into line the last straggler. The
cry of the Crusade may not have been audibly uttered,
but it certainly kept ringing in the conscience, 'The
Lord wills it.' The spontaneous praise service was an
appropriate conclusion to the campaign.

"Any account of our recent struggle omitting to
mention the share of the consecrated women in it,
would be sadly defective. They did everything *but
vote.* They made personal appeals, and were instant in
prayer.

"The local Union of the Woman's Christian Temperance Union formed a happy nucleus, around which
the elect ladies gathered, thus again proving itself a
providential agency. Next to the Church we esteem
the Woman's Christian Temperance Union, the most
thoroughly-organized and efficient philanthropic society
of our times."

A continuous prayer-meeting, March 14, 1887,
in the Methodist Episcopal Church was held in
support of the efforts at the polls, and the lunch
at the City Hall was free to all voters! Of this

meeting our secretary, Mrs. Maggie L. Gregg,
says:

"There was a Presence whose manifestations and influence could be felt upon entering the room. The
'God of Jacob' in whom the old Crusaders trusted, and
into whose ear the prayers of thousands of women
have been received in the past thirteen years, was
there, whispering the assuring words: 'Said I not, if
thou wouldst believe thou shouldst see the glory of
God?'"

The polls closed at five o'clock, and as we
lingered to hear the last report, it was proposed
that when our victory should be assured, the bells
must ring out the praise of God, beginning with
a few taps from the bell of the "Old Crusade
Church!" As the crowd dispersed, an announce-
ment was made by the ministers for a praise-
meeting at 7.30 in the Methodist Episcopal
Church. And thus the hilariousness of the people found a glorious channel in songs of victory
and prayers of thanksgiving.

XXI.

FROM the time of the Dow Law victory, March
14, 1887, little occurred of special interest
in the Crusade work of Hillsboro. Everything
tended to a well-defined battle between good

laws and bad execution on the part of the community of voters and their officers,—a battle in
which women were powerless; but gospel temperance meetings were continued, the children
were not forgotten, temperance literature was
distributed, the prisoners were visited, and the
weekly Woman's Christian Temperance Union
prayer-meetings were never omitted.

At one of these services, about the 12th of
September, 1887, it was intimated that a carriage was at the door awaiting me for a service
that required my attention, quite out of town.
In my absence the meeting was continued,
and a *secret plan* was formed for celebrating
the coming anniversary of *our Golden Wedding*.
The Rev. Davis W. Clark was foremost in aiding the ladies in developing this plan. The
story of this occasion will be found, as told by
our former secretary, Mrs. D. K. Fenner, in the
chapter contributed by my daughter, Marie T.
Rives; but I may be permitted here to say of
this beautiful occasion, that it remains to my
husband and myself one of the most cherished
memories of our lives. Having just passed the
"golden milestone," and having served our local
Union for *thirteen* years as president, I began to
feel that a younger woman might be more
efficient.

My resignation was referred to a committee

(Mrs. Rev. W. J. McSurely and Mrs. Maggie L. Gregg), who replied as follows :

"Your committee, to whom was submitted Mrs. Thompson's request that she be released from the presidency of our local Union, would respectfully submit: That we do not consider Mrs. Thompson 'superannuated ;' that, although often prevented from meeting with us, yet when she is present we do not perceive that her natural force is abated ; and we know that we but voice the feeling of all in saying that we most earnestly desire that she, who first led us out in this work, may continue to be our president for many years to come. We submit this, not as a mere sentiment, but from a conviction that we are doing what is best for our Union. Feeling that *God* called Mrs. Thompson to be our leader, we await a clearer indication of Providence that another is to take her place.

"In the mean time, during her absence from us, we recognize another leader in our first vice-president, Mrs. Hart, and we will faithfully stand by her."

The matter being thus adjusted, Mrs. Hart, with her usual energy and earnestness, prepared an appeal to the mayor and Council of our town, and, accompanied by Mesdames Foraker, McSurely, Murray, Smith, Gregg, Langley, Bridwell, Patterson, Willett, Stevenson, and McConnaughy, delivered it at the set time, and was sustained by two of the councilmen, Dr. Patterson and Mr. McNichol, with eloquent and earnest speeches favoring their wishes.   Mrs. Hart's appeal is worth reading, notwithstanding the majority was against us:

"To the Hon. Mayor and Council of Hillsboro:

"It is claimed that the ordinance prohibiting the sale of intoxicating liquor in our town is but a dead letter upon our statute-books, and feeling aggrieved that this is so, we, the women of Hillsboro, through the Woman's Christian Temperance Union, come to you with an earnest appeal to see to it that it be enforced. Nearly two years ago this ordinance was asked for by more than two-thirds of our voters, and by our united voice. It was placed upon our statute-books, not as a pastime, not as empty words, but to be enforced just as any law, and, as affecting our interests more than any law, you are asked to enforce, as by its non-enforcement our homes, our happiness, and the souls of our loved ones are placed in jeopardy. The voters, who asked its adoption, expected you, as sworn officers of the law, to enforce it. We hear it said that the ordinance is a failure. We grant that its enforcement has been a failure, but the ordinance is right, and right can not be wrong. It may need revision to make it more effective, and we pray your honorable body to do this. Can you turn a deaf ear to our appeal? We also ask that you make an appropriation of money sufficient to enable our officers to execute the law.

"On behalf of the Woman's Christian Temperance Union of Hillsboro, Ohio,   MRS. GOV. HART,

"Acting Pres., First Vice-Pres.

" LIZZIE H. HARSHA, *Secretary.*"

All this effort on the part of the temperance women and their friends so stirred up matters, that the "powers that be" determined to enforce the "tax" part of the "Dow Law," and let them sell on, as they had been doing (without paying for the "privilege"). With the money thus collected our streets, "so wide and airy," were vigorously macadamized, and thus, while the tempted ones were drawn into the "open doors," the "very rocks were crying out" against "those people who love to have it so." "And what will ye do in the end thereof?" has been asked, not only by the prophet, but by many aching hearts, since that day, for "at last it stingeth like an adder," even "our enemies themselves being judges."

XXII.

FEBRUARY 27, 1889, Mrs. Hart suggested a temperance dinner by the Woman's Christian Temperance Union, as one had not been given for some time, and the treasury was getting low. Ample preparations were made, and, March 2d, the dinner was given in the city hall. It was well patronized, and gave great satisfaction; but, best of all, it left a good impression, socially as well as financially.

The family and large connection of Mr. and Mrs. H. S. Foraker had planned so quietly and successfully in their preparations for their fiftieth

anniversary of the wedding-day, that the Woman's Christian Temperance Union came very
near being excluded; but the secret was found
out in time to send the following: An exquisite
banneret in white and gold, from the co-workers
of the Woman's Christian Temperance Union,
with the inscription:

1839.   *1889.*

Golden Wedding.

Congratulations

from

The W. C. T. U. of Hillsboro,

to

Mr. and Mrs. H. S. Foraker.

May each coming milestone of life's journey prove
a fresh Ebenezer until the golden gate is reached!

For our dear sister of Crusade memory the words of
the Master seem most fitting:

"O woman, great is thy faith!"

About this time it was the pleasure of our
Union to respond to the call of Miss Pugh, national treasurer, and send our contribution and
loving sentiments to Frances E. Willard, the one
we all "delighted to honor," and especially as
she approached the end of her "fifty successful
years."

From the minutes we find that "a memorial
service in honor of the late Mrs. Hayes was
held in the Methodist Episcopal Church, under

the direction of the Woman's Christian Temperance Union. Mrs. Thompson presided, Dr.
McSurely read the Scriptures, and Rev. King, of
the Baptist Church, led in prayer. The remarks
of Mrs. Thompson were very appropriate and
touching, and she paid a fine tribute to Ex-
President Hayes for his loyalty to his wife in
supporting her in her heroic stand for sobriety
in the White House. Mrs. Hart and Mrs. Murray read very excellent papers, and Mrs. Rives
gave a thoughtful and happily-worded address.
Mrs. D. S. Ferguson read an original poem, and
Mrs. Wm. Gregg read a poem prepared by Mr.
J. L. Boardman. The whole affair was most
happily conceived and carried out. The papers,
addresses, and poems were in excellent taste,
and show a tender appreciation of the noble
Christian woman, whose courage and truth have
entitled her to the respect and love of the Christian world. The services were closed with the
benediction by Rev. Murray."

The semi-annual meeting of the Woman's
Christian Temperance Union of Highland
County was held in the Methodist Episcopal
Church of this place, May, 1889. Delegates were
present from five Unions in the county, and were
welcomed by Mrs. Dr. McSurely in behalf of the
Hillsboro Union.

Mrs. Caroline B. Buell, national corresponding secretary, was with us by invitation, and addressed a large evening meeting in the Methodist Episcopal Church, and also led a very profitable service on the following morning in the old Crusade Church. She gave much satisfaction, and with many of our citizens is a standing favorite.

Mrs. Alphonso, Hart at this Convention resigned her office as county president, much to the regret of all parties interested, her husband, Hon. Alphonso Hart, having been appointed to an office that required the removal of his family to Washington, D. C. We were deprived also of her services in our local work; this we felt a very great loss. Mrs. McSurely was appointed vice-president in Mrs. Hart's place from the Presbyterian Church, and Mrs. Mary B. Murray, first vice-president from the Methodist Episcopal Church for the local Union.

About this time, November 23, 1889, Mr. George Woodford, of national fame, came by invitation of the Woman's Christian Temperance Union, to give Hillsboro a week of his temperance zeal and eloquence. Much good resulted; but as our secretary, Mrs. Charles Harsha, says in her minutes, "We can never know the result Mr. Woodford's meetings until we all meet at the judgment seat where the men and youths of this town must face the God of justice, in the

presence of the man who tried so hard to save
them from a fate worse than death."

Mrs. Mary B. Murray, president of the Y's and
a kind and efficient aid to the Woman's Christian
Temperance Union, was about this time, December 1, 1889, induced, at the earnest request of Mrs.
E. J. Thompson, to accept the position of president *pro tem.* during a season of severe illness in
her family.   Thus seconded by her good husband,
Rev. James Murray, pastor of the Methodist
Episcopal Church, when the bugle-note from our
chieftain, Miss Willard, sounded the call for a
"Crusade camp-fire" in Hillsboro, December
23, 1889, to celebrate the fifteenth anniversary,
they were "willing" and earnest, and, together
with other faithful and tried White Ribboners in
the Crusade town and the State, the work moved
forward.

The "camp-fire" of December, 1889, at the
"Old Fort" of the Crusade, was a vigorous
demonstration, and at this late day memory
seems to bring out in clear-cut outline our dear
chieftain, with her inspiring presence and " wonderful words."   Miss Elizabeth Scoville, whose
"Bible-readings" are still treasured as inspired
and helpful through so many years, was here
from her Southern home, and Anna Gordon, the
beloved "indispensable," whom our children love
to remember.   Then we had the faithful Sunday

Observance National Superintendent Mrs. Ba-
teum; also Mrs. Peters, the generous donor of the
beautiful *and useful* " Crusade Bible-case." But
the executive power behind the throne (and often
upon it) was our own unselfish State president,
Mrs. Monroe. She came to our rescue with wise
plans, and being, with Mrs. Clevenger, State corresponding secretary, guests of Rev. and Mrs.
Murray, they combined, with our own workers,
to make the occasion equal to Miss Willard's
highest anticipations.

These retrospective views are instructive; but
what shall we say of the " harvest " which is now
"white for the reapers;" of the noble English
woman of titled distinction, whose heart hath
been touched, to bring in such rich grain and
stately sheaves for the Master? The tender association that exists between our own Frances E.
Willard and Lady Henry Somerset, to my mind,
is a sure indication of God's special care and
helpfulness in the "battle" that is "not ours,"
but "His."

I, who sit and watch, in my *eightieth year*, the
work going on in this great " harvest-field," and
catch glimpses of inspiration from the " white
ribbons " that gleam " around the world," and
especially across the ocean blue, at the great
London Convention, feel my grasp loosen upon
the busy laborers; yet quietly and peacefully

the faith that *inspired* and has sustained this movement, which is " not of ourselves but the gift of God," grows more steadfast in the ultimate result—of self-sacrifice and sobriety.

IV.

MY MOTHER'S YEARS APPROACHING LIFE'S SUNSET.

IV.

MY MOTHER'S YEARS APPROACHING LIFE'S SUNSET.

" Faces looking into the sunset are golden."
—F. W. Faber.

TO write of the years of one who descends the hill of life as gracefully and bravely as my mother, is a theme for a more capable pen than mine; but the daughter's hand that so often placed the "old arm-chair," that in pride arranged the fleecy white becoming cap and graceful shawl; the heart that always throbbed in sympathy with the " White Ribbon," and had cozy, loving chats over the fireside about home interests, and domestic occupations, is perhaps the one to follow her gently down life's decline.   We often said to each other, too,

" So many links have softly
        Dropped from sight,
So many names are now in
Sadness spoken,—names
        Once so bright."

The beginning of my mother's approaching sunset years brought me to a period in my own life when bereavement caused me to change homes, and return a widow to reside with and assist my parents during their declining years. Mother had lived through many sorrows and bereavements of her eventful life, and my heart often found solace in her love and tender sympathy.

Years had passed since she led the heroic temperance band forward that bleak winter morning, in Hillsboro, Ohio (December 23, 1873), and broke the snow and ice, not only of weather, but also public opinion, and inaugurated the Ohio Woman's Crusade,—

> " That pleading voice rose calm and sweet
>   From woman's earnest tongue,
>   And Riot turned her scowling glance,
>   Awed from her tranquil countenance."

The "sober after-thought" of this great movement had crystallized into the "Woman's Christian Temperance Union," and mother's temperance work now was the presidency of the Hillsboro Union, attending National and State Conventions, a correspondence in all parts of our own and other countries with the temperance workers, and the highest work her prayers for the cause and the laborers.

Neither my mother's face, manner, nor disposition had changed much to me with the flight

of years. My earliest recollection of her was that she was very cheerful, and I thought beautiful. She had to me a poetic face, something like Mrs. Sigourney's—such soft brown eyes and lovely curls. I remember once, when I was a young girl away from home (and I suspect home-sick), I purchased a beautiful jewel, and searched in vain for the "gold-stone" that looked like mother's eyes, which the jeweler failed to find to my satisfaction. My sketch is only a brief recital of a few incidents of a remarkable descent of life. Mother would shrink from allowing the world to know her best attributes and most unselfish acts; but when her "works follow her," many appreciative pens will call her "blessed."

The old home which had been the residence of my parents, Judge and Mrs. Thompson, since their removal from "Dewy Lawn," my father's beautiful residence in my childhood, was an inheritance of my mother from her father, Governor Trimble, having been her parents' home, and built by her father.

> " More dear, as years on years advance,
> We prize the old inheritance,
> And feel, as far and wide we roam,
> That all we seek we have at home."

It had all the old landmarks when I returned again to it, and the combination of my furniture, pictures, rugs, and smaller treasures added com-

fort and beauty to the rooms, already handsomely
furnished with old-time and modern furniture.
Partly from taste, and also for convenience, my
parents selected for their room the back parlor with
a northern view and indoor passage-way to the
dining-room; for the old home was built with
the general entrance to the dining-room from a
southern porch, and although in the summer the
view, the vines, and the green grass made it
charming, when the winter storms came, delicate
persons needed cloaks, and indeed sometimes
umbrellas had a mission; and only that we knew
in the Southern States, the kitchens were sometimes so far removed from the house that the
hot buckwheat cakes were carried on horseback
to the dining-room, could we feel our architecture
had made wonderful strides. But the lack of
convenience in the old home was more than
atoned for by the large, hospitable halls and
rooms, and by the sacred memories and echo of
silent footsteps, which made the old Southern
porch especially dear; for all loved it. The little
birds sang their first sweet spring carols near its
low windows, and sought shelter from the winter storms in the bushes near the dining-room
door. There had been much hospitality in all
the years past in the old home, but, as the years
of my mother's life increased, came bereavements in quick succession, oftentimes also fam-

ily illness, curtailing the usual entertainments; but the latch-string was always out, and a guest was no innovation.

That my father's charming sisters could so seldom visit Hillsboro of late years has been a family regret, and a cherished memory is the last visit of Mrs. Maria Daviess, with her daughter Anna; my father's sister, and school-mate in youth, of whose talent Kentucky is so proud, whose heart is as gentle as the south wind, and whose face is also turned to the golden sunset.

Among the guests at the old home, none afforded my mother more pleasure than Miss Frances E. Willard and charming Miss Anna Gordon. They visited us several times in the interests of their work, and Miss Willard addressed large temperance audiences, and the people were permitted to hear the peer of woman speakers. Mother loved to call Miss Willard her dear daughter and leader; and after her mother passed to the "Home over there," the affectionate appreciation was even more dear to the great and good and lovely woman, the leader of us all. Other prominent temperance workers were my mother's guests,—the lamented Mrs. Woodbridge, and Ohio's president, Mrs. Monroe; and secretary, Mrs. Clevenger; and Mrs. Perkins, of Cleveland; and Mrs. Hunt, of Boston; Mrs. Yeomans, of Canada,—all so dear to the cause, and heart of their hostess. I was the only child at home when the approaching sunset years brought the Golden Wedding. The description I insert from the report of Mrs. D. K. Fenner, written for the *Union Signal.*

Let our first secretary, Mrs. Mary B. Fenner, tell the story, as appointed by the Hillsboro Woman's Christian Temperance Union for the *Union Signal,* September 28, 1887:

" Some friendly little bird having whispered that the Golden Wedding was at hand, the idea suggested itself to the members of the Woman's Christian Temperance Union that here was a fitting and delightful opportunity of testifying their affectionate appreciation of Mrs. Thompson's unflinching devotion to the cause, typified in all its ramifications by the white ribbon, as also their personal esteem and respect; the outgrowth of thirteen years' intercourse and companionship in the work of putting down intemperance, during all of which time she has been the honored president of the local Union.

" Ideas soon take form when hands and hearts work together, and in a few days little white-winged messengers were flying over the length and breadth of the land, bidding guests to the Golden Wedding.

" The list of invitations included the Crusaders, signers of the Guarantee Fund, members of the Hillsboro bar, mayor and city officials, officers of the Churches, the Young Woman's Christian Temperance Union, State presidents, and National officers of the Woman's Christian Temperance Union, in all about four hundred and fifty.

" The reception was given in the Methodist Episcopal Church, and on the appointed evening, September 21st, a large and elegant assemblage gathered in the audience-room. Brave men and fair women were there, but the admiration and interest of all the goodly company were centered on the little bride and her tall and still handsome husband.

" Seated on the platform with Judge and Mrs. Thompson were Rev. D. W. Clark, pastor of the Church; Rev. Dr. Ketcham, late pastor of the same; Rev. W. J. McSurely, of the Presbyterian Church; Mrs. Monroe, president of the State Union; Mrs. Clevenger, corresponding secretary of the same; Mrs. Hart, vice-president of the local Union, and several of the older members of the Union.

" Rev. W. J. McSurely, who presided at the first Crusade meeting, occupied the chair on this occasion. His cordial congratulations were responded to by Judge Thompson in a most characteristic speech, genial, poetical, and touching.

" Mrs. Hart's address on behalf of the local Union was short, but gem-like in its perfect finish, pure color, and chaste setting.

" Mrs. Henrietta L. Monroe, of Xenia, president of the State Union, followed in an address of rare elegance, strength, and beauty. She gave a brief outline of the origin of the Crusade, the organization of the Woman's Christian Temperance Union, and its present widespread influence and working power. No one who heard her could fail to be impressed with the importance and influence of the White-ribbon organization, and of the immensity of the work it is doing.

" Mrs. Monroe closed with a touching and eloquent tribute to Mrs. Thompson, and then presented to her, on

behalf of the National Woman's Christian Temperance
Union, a testimonial, engrossed in gold on vellum, and
framed in gold and antique oak.   The reader will at once
recognize Miss Willard's facile pen:

"'1837–1887. Headquarters Woman's Christian Temperance Union, Chicago, Ill., to Mrs. Eliza Trimble
Thompson, of Hillsboro, Ohio, leader of the first Praying
Band in the Woman's Temperance Crusade, on the occasion of her Golden Wedding, September 21, 1887.'

"'To have been the first woman who ever attended a
National Temperance Convention; to have led the pioneer
band in that heroic movement of which the National Woman's Christian Temperance Union is the organic form;
to have made Hillsboro known to the world as the cradle
of the Crusade ; to have impressed your name upon the
history of your country,—all this is much; but to have
worn so loyally the crown of daughter, sister, wife, and
mother; to have won friends, wherever the sacred cause
of temperance is loved, and to have exhibited in public
life and home's sweet ministries a faith

> " That when in darkness knows no fear,
>   In danger feels no doubt,"

is more. You stand upon the heights of answered
prayer, and we, your comrades, whom your unwavering
cheerfulness has many times animated, wave to you
from the plain and thickest of the fight our

"God bless you and yours on this auspicious day."

"'In Behalf of the W. C. T. U., etc.'"

"After the reading of this testimonial, Mrs. Monroe
unveiled Ohio's offering; at the sight of which a mur-
mur of delighted surprise ran through the house.   It
was a tall urn, Etruscan in shape, of gold bronze, ex-

quisitely chased and hammered. Suspended by a gold
chain from the handle is a twenty-dollar gold-piece,
bearing on the obverse side the inscription, '1837–1887,
Mrs. Eliza J. Thompson, leader of the Crusade, from the
Ohio Woman's Christian Temperance Union.' On the
reverse, an engraved representation of the Crusade
Church with the date ' December 23, 1873.'

" Mrs. Thompson's response to these tributes of loving
congratulation was made in her usual quiet, conversa-
tional manner, and showed her appreciation of the ovation given her, but she confessed herself dazed and be-
wildered with surprise, and said: 'The bride should not
be expected to do too much at the wedding.'

" The pastor of the Church, Rev. D. W. Clark, read the
congratulatory telegrams. They had come from nearly
every State and Territory in the Union, and all bore most
kindly greetings.

"At the close of these formal exercises the invited
guests repaired to the lecture-room, where they were
seated and served with refreshments, in number about
one hundred. At the close of the banquet, Rev. D. W.
Clark, on behalf of Mrs. Marie Thompson Rives, presented to the Hillsboro bar a full-length, life-size portrait of her father. It was unveiled by Mrs. Sarah
Thompson Collins, the granddaughter of Judge Thompson, and accepted on behalf of the bar by Hon. Alphonso
Hart, in a pleasant, cordial, and appropriate speech.

" Then followed the reading of a beautiful poem by
J. L. Boardman, Esq., an address and reading of letters
by Mrs. Antoinette H. Clevenger, the reading of letters
from former pastors and presiding elders, and more telegrams. Among the gifts were noticeable several little
satin purses of blue and white, on which, in letters of
gold were the words: ' Our testimonial, Maryland

W. C. T. U.;' 'Our testimonial, New Hampshire W. C.
T. U.;' 'Our testimonial, New Jersey W. C. T. U.,'
'Our testimonial, Pastors and Elders, Hillsboro M. E.
Church;' 'Our testimonial, W. C. T. U.' These contained (in various amounts—gold pieces) the cash
value of checks sent by the several State Unions whose
names they bear, and for whom the time was too short
to allow of sending a testimonial in any other form.

"At the close of the evening many old friends, one of
whom, Judge William Meek, had been a guest at the
first wedding, fifty years before, pressed forward to express personally to Judge and Mrs. Thompson their congratulations, and wishes for both a long, happy, and useful future."

The congratulations and gifts of many rela-
tives and prominent social friends were received,
none more appreciated than the golden lamp
from Mrs. Rufus King, and the "History of
Prussia," in which is inscribed: "To James H.
and Eliza J. Thompson, from Herbert Tuttle."

My mother's fine qualities as a nurse, of patience, attention, and tenderness, can be testified
to by physicians, husband, children, parents, and
many to whom she ministered as "unto Him."
Months of frail health and delicate strength kept
her near me, and the days were cheerful because
of her devotion, and "never can I forget her
sweet glances cast upon me when I appeared
asleep; never her kiss of peace at night." Her
family physician and nephew, Dr. Henry M.
Brown, often called her "the General" because

of her fine executive qualities, and Dr. W. W.
Glenn, of Hillsboro, and other physicians appreciated her disposition of endurance and helpfulness in the sick-room.

Apparently she bore separation by death with
unusual heart-fortitude; but it was unselfish, for
the sake of others. Every family death changed
her, and broke her heroic spirit. "Kisses became more holy, and partings touched the soul
to deeper woe."

She often talked to me about the many family bereavements, and told me of her "blessed
dreams" that her angel children welcomed her
home, when she would retire "weary of earth,"
and, perhaps, physically a little ill. She ever
misses the companionship of her gifted, first-born
son, Allen T. Thompson, one of the heroes of
life, made great by suffering and triumph, and his
Christian victories stimulated her own Christian
walk and zeal. "Gentle Anna's" lovely life and
death are a vision of beauty which always dim
her spectacles to talk about; and the California
mementos of dear brother Joseph break her
down completely, as do dear Sarah's little treasures; and names so dear to her widowed daughters are always sacred to her.

Although her parents both passed away at a
very advanced age, her memories and conversation about them have all the freshness and sin-

cerity of the request, "Make me a child again,
just for to-night," as she tells us, in the evenings,
around the cheerful fireside and bright lamp, of
their devotion and munificence towards her. She
ever misses her brothers, and feels stricken as
she stands the only one left of the large family circle.

My mother was a delegate-at-large to all the National and Ohio State Conventions of the Woman's
Christian Temperance Union, and her presence
was called a benediction, and her characteristic
and earnest speeches much appreciated. She
was always honored by Miss Willard, the National and State officers, and all the workers; and
she returned home invigorated in health, and
strengthened in spiritual life to labor.

She greatly enjoys a personal acquaintance
with Lady Henry Somerset, England's great
leader and White Ribbon temperance advocate,
whose gifts and social graces win all hearts.

Rev. Thomas J. Melish and Rev. Peter Tins-
ley, D. D., were guests at our home during an
Episcopal Convocation. These prominent cler-
gymen spoke of her unusual cheerfulness and
vivacity, and how well life's lessons had been
learned by her and imparted to others.

Although one of the most devoted Meth-
odists of her age, in early life having imbibed

from her grandmother, Jane Trimble, all the
zeal of pioneer Christianity, in her later years
the distance of her home from the church, much
sickness in the family, and oftentimes her own
delicate health, curtails her public worship. Her
home spirit of patience, self-denial, and cheerfulness about it, makes her own soul expand,
and through her example, that of others; and
who can tell but in the closet, with closed doors,
when she would fain be at Church, her prayers
do more to build up Christ's kingdom than un-
interrupted Church attendance? She attends as
faithfully as possible her Sunday afternoon class-
meeting, and always finds comfort and help from
her class-leader and friend, Mr. Chaney. Rev.
Dr. Marlay says of her: "As Mrs. Thompson's
pastor for three years, I had every opportunity
to study her religious character and understand
it. I esteemed her as one of the most efficient
helpers, and as one of the noblest and most devoted Christian women I had ever known. How
much, and in how many ways, she has helped
her pastors and her Church, eternity alone can
reveal. Others, doubtless, will speak more fully
of her connection with the ever-memorable Crusade. That work, it seems to me, must forever
stand as the crowning glory of her life; for un-
doubtedly it was a divine inspiration; and it

was moreover, as I believe, the most effective
and far-reaching temperance movement the world
has ever seen."

Morning prayer is a regular service at our
home, conducted by mother, and her prayers will
be a sacred legacy to her children.

It is difficult to class her occupations, even in
later years; for she has always been a busy
woman,—housekeeping and all home interests
always faithfully and successfully attended to ;
sewing and knitting, which, with her, are accom-
plishments as well as occupations; general reading; diligent Bible study; a large family, general and temperance correspondence ; social calls
at home and upon old acquaintances. She is
very fond of her neighbors, and appreciates, as
much as any one I ever knew, greetings of dear
friends, and sweet children, and faithful domes-
tics. Her cheerfulness, humor, and sympathetic
qualities endear her to all classes.

My mother's religious interest in the colored
people, and their devotion to her, is genuine.

Her later years have been much helped over
the cares of domestic life by the faithfulness and
efficiency of those who have lived with her for
many years.

Several years after my return to the old home,
my brother Henry came from Colorado, where he
had been living, to visit his parents, who prevailed

upon him to give up business prospects away from home, and remain to cheer and aid the small family circle.

Both my brothers, Henry B. and John B. Thompson, of Salt Lake City, have added much serenity to the declining years of my parents by their devotion and helpfulness. One noble grandson, George A. Thompson, of Xenia, Ohio, his lovely family and mother, Mrs. Allen Thompson, are a source of affectionate interest and pride.

When bereavement broke up Mrs. Herbert Tuttle's charming "Cornell" home, "sister Mary arranged her life to pass a part of the time with her parents, and to solace herself by home sympathy and companionship, and the old home has again what it has so long missed—her society and artistic taste.

Time deals gently with my dear father also, whose declining years are unusually vigorous, mentally and physically. My parents' devotion to each other needs no pen to herald it; and no home scene comes closer to my heart than to see them in the evening of life still together, and with so much left them to enjoy.

Occasionally June roses bring family reunions of unusual pleasure, when the devoted sisters of many years, Mrs. Joseph Trimble and my mother, can weave in conversation a tapestry of loving memories; and the attractive nieces, who love and admire Aunt "Eliza," flit through the old halls and rooms, sweet with the precious perfume, and tender echo of "Auld Lang Syne."

As I close these pages, the summer of 1895 is bringing my mother's seventy-ninth birthday. The rich temperance fruitage brought together the great London Convention of June, which Miss Frances E. Willard says is the outcome of the inspired work of the Crusade.

That my mother could not attend the London Convention and accept the hospitality of Lady Henry Somerset was a mutual regret, as the resolution passed at Queen's Hall during the World's Convention attests:

"*Resolved*, That we rejoice in the presence of our beloved Mother Stewart, and applaud the courage that led her to cross the sea in her eightieth year that she might impart to us the inspiration of her presence and her voice.

"That to Mrs. Judge Thompson, of Hillsboro, Ohio, leader of the first Prayer Band, we hereby send the assurance that we have missed her gentle and womanly presence, and that the Crusade Bible and Crusade Psalm have been to us hallowed reminders of the brave stand she took when she was called to lead the women of Hillsboro, Ohio, in the great Crusade now known and felt the world around."

December, 1895, will bring the twenty-second anniversary of the Ohio Crusade. The snow will fall gently where noble workers are at rest.

" Flashing o'er the pathway white," the mighty
work will go on, and in quiet homes the Mother
Leaders will look out upon the scene, where
Right is growing stronger, and " Righteousness
that exalteth a nation " is spreading more rapidly
because of woman's courage and faithful prayers.

V.

MY FRIEND MRS. THOMPSON

And the Present Condition of the Temperance Work,

BY

FRANCES E. WILLARD.

13

V.

EVERY whirlwind has its first leaf; for the laws of motion oblige it to begin somewhere in particular. Other leaves are gathered in so rapidly that it is usually impossible to tell which one stirred first; but whichever that one was, with it the whirlwind began.

The "Ohio Crusade" has passed into history; the "Ohio Crusaders" have won an inextinguishable fame. The "Women of the West" who led the "Whisky War," as it is called throughout the British Empire, gained for themselves, without intending it, the pioneer place in that great Woman's Temperance Movement that now belts the globe. The whirlwind of the Lord began in the little town of Hillsboro, on the 23d of December, 1873. There the Pentecost of God descended, and seventy women, without the slightest preconcerted plan, lifted their hands as silent witnesses, when asked by the good ministers and the famous lecturer if they were willing to go out from their homes and pray in the places where their husbands, sons, and brothers were tempted to

their ruin. There the Crusade Psalm was read ; a
rallying cry, "Give to the winds thy fears," was
sung ; and the first silent, prayerful procession of
wives and mothers moved along Ohio streets.
The gentle-hearted woman whom they chose as
their leader by spontaneous acclamation was one
whose heart had been mellowed by glorious discipline and sorrow.   Away back in 1836, she had
accompanied her father, then an Ohio delegate
to the National Temperance Convention held in
Saratoga, New York, and when, at his request,
she went with him to the door of the hotel dining-room, which afforded ample accommodation
for all the delegates in that rudimentary period
of the movement, and he asked her to enter with
him, Eliza Thompson, who was a girl of but
twenty years, naturally hesitated, saying to her
stout-hearted sire : "Why, father, I am afraid to
go in.   I looked through the door, and there were
no women present, only men."   Upon this the
governor exclaimed: "Come right along with
me ; my daughter must never be afraid in a good
cause !"   And taking her by the arm, he introduced the first woman who ever entered a National Temperance Convention in the United
States.   Who shall say that in this scene—how
much more worthy of a painter than most of the
subjects that they choose !—we have not a prophecy of what was to transpire nearly forty years

later in the town of that sweet girl's nativity?
Ancestry counts for much, and it should never
be forgotten in our study of heredity, that the
leader of the Crusade came of a long line of devout Christian ancestors, whose earlier history
dated back to Virginia, that famous State which
was the home of George Washington, and is
known in history as the " Mother of Presidents."

The first time that I ever saw Mrs. Judge
Thompson she was seated on the platform on the
right of Mrs. Jane Fowler Willing, the president
of the Convention in Cleveland, November, 1874,
at which the National Woman's Christian Temperance Union was organized. I came to the
Convention from Evanston, Illinois, where I had
resigned a professorship in the Northwestern
University, only a few months before. Never
having been a temperance worker, I had no knowledge of the persons of the Crusade save such as
an intelligent reader was able to gather from the
current press. Of Mrs. Thompson and Mother
Stewart I had heard; but I had no prevision as
to who was entitled to the high honor of being
called the leader of the first Praying Band of the
Crusade. But in Cleveland this question was
settled for all time. While Mother Stewart was
applauded as "a burning and shining light,"
whose natural gifts of speech and dauntless
bravery would forever make her a central figure

in the Crusade picture, it was taken as a matter
of course that the quiet, low-voiced, motherly little
woman on the platform was " first in war " even
as she has always been "first in peace." It was
freely said, that in Washington Court-house,
where the Crusade broke out the day following
its manifestation in Hillsboro, greater results
were reached, and that hence the fire spread
with a steady flame; but the women of Hillsboro were " in at the birth," and Hillsboro is the
cradle, even as Washington Court-house is the
crown, of the Crusade.

So far as I can learn, the women of Hillsboro
put forward no claim, nor did their leader. Perhaps this was because there was no need for them
to do so ; and to my mind, the strongest confirma-
tion of their deserved pre-eminence is the quiet,
gentle, peace-making spirit that they have shown
from the beginning. For my part, I can testify
that it has only been "by the hardest" that her
comrades have been able to induce Mrs. Thompson to come forward and gently take her place
as "leader of the first Praying Band." On some
notable occasions this typical woman of the
home, the Church, and school has stood forth as
a historic figure. Who of us whose lot has been
cast as an officer or delegate to the National Convention since the beginning, can forget the genial,
smiling presence and piquant words of that Cru-

sade mother whom we all love so much? To
hear her tell the story of the way in which the
movement broke out in Hillsboro is an experience to be cherished for a lifetime. Her quaint,
refined presence; her mild, motherly face, framed
in its little cap; her soft voice; her peculiar
manner of utterance, combining remarkable
originality with the utmost gentleness and good
breeding; her inimitable humor; and, most characteristic of all, her deep, abiding faith in God
and in humanity,—all these have made an indel-
ible impression, and helped, beyond what we can
at all estimate, to form the character of the White
Ribbon Movement. Naturally of a conservative
disposition, Mrs. Thompson has, nevertheless,
kept time to the company's music; she has taken
every wave of the onrolling tide of impulse that
we believe to be from God, as a strong swimmer
breasts the incoming waves of the sea. It was
no trifle for a woman with the traditions of "Old
Virginia" to accept our woman's suffrage resolution away back in 1877; and the beauty of it
was, that her manner of announcing the faith
that was within her lent so much of quiet strength
to the decision of the Convention. It was the
same when we avowed our fealty to the Prohibition party in 1884, and when, at Cleveland recently, the proposition was put forward to have
a vice-president-at-large, who should represent

the president in her absence. Although twenty
years had passed since the Crusade, her "eye was
not dimmed nor her natural force abated;" and
I never have known a Convention more amused,
convinced, unified, than by her inimitable little
speech upon that question.

At this distance it can do no harm to refer to
the incident that accompanied the lamented departure of a dozen good women, headed by one
who was at that time a well-known leader in our
councils. I refer to the non-partisan exodus in
Battery D, Chicago, at the Annual Convention of
1889. When these sisters, thirteen in number,
out of a Convention of four hundred or there-
abouts, retired from the scene, I asked if there
were not other women from Iowa, the State that
had contributed most of the departing delegates,
who would fill up the vacancies; and from forty
to fifty Hawkeye White Ribboners crowded forward amid the plaudits of the Convention. Mary
T. Lathrap then rose, and, with her usual dignity
and grace, offered a resolution of respect and regret, which was unanimously adopted; after which
Mrs. Thompson came forward, it being now
late at night, later indeed than a woman of her
age should have been out at a public meeting—
and I dare say the like had never happened her
before, and never will again—and, with a gesture
of mingled drollery and pathos, threw around my

shoulders the shawl she had worn in the Crusade
procession, and standing beside me called on the
delegates to rally.   It was one of the most inspired moments that I have ever witnessed.   The
whole Convention rose, crowding together, and
we sang the song that Mother Thompson—for so
we love to call her in these later years—had
given out when the first Praying Band moved
forward:

"Give to the winds thy fears."

Best of all, this dramatic action was wholly un-
premeditated.   Mother Thompson had brought
the shawl to give it to me as a surprise; she had
no idea that our sisters contemplated leaving us;
but she is that kind of a woman. She has her forces
well in hand; she is imperturbable; as Garfield
said of his true-hearted wife, "She is unstam-
pedeable."   This great quality is not only in-
herited and innate, but comes of the culture of a
lifetime in "the peace of God that passeth understanding."

It was my good fortune, as far back as 1876,
to make a tour among the Crusaders of Ohio,
visiting well-nigh forty of their towns and vil-
lages.   I could write a volume on the history,
experience, and inspiration of that memorable
pilgrimage.   It was one of the few times in my
life that I ever went forth alone; and I was
mothered in the homes of those devoted women

with a tenderness that will never be forgotten. My own stipulation in making the trip was that I should go to Hillsboro, the home of Mrs. Thompson, and to Springfield, the home of Mother Stewart, in both of which we took sweet counsel together.

Mrs. Thompson's home is the old family mansion where the governor spent all his days, and which he bequeathed to his beloved only daughter. It stands on a slight ascent and in a wooded grove, at the edge of a well-built town of four thousand inhabitants, and is roomy and hospitable as heart could wish. Here I met Judge Thompson, the genial, witty lawyer, and husband of our leader; Mrs. Marie Thompson Rives, the accomplished elder daughter; and Henry Thompson, the youth who brought the tidings to his mother that she was expected at the church on that memorable morning. I longed to see that lovely younger daughter, who from her pocket Bible brought to her mother the Crusade Psalm, that is the Magna Charta of the White Ribbon Movement; but she was gone, having been married to Herbert Tuttle, the distinguished professor in Cornell University, Ithaca, New York.

Those were delightful days in that happy home. We visited the famous Crusade Church, and made the acquaintance of its pastor, the

Rev. Dr. McSurely, who befriended the women from first to last in all their work. We held meetings in the basement of his church, where the first Crusade Praying Band convened; we read the Crusade Psalm from the old Bible, and sang the Crusade hymn. And I have now in my den at home, given me by dear Mrs. Thompson, a relic of the Crusade days from a Hillsboro saloon, one of the first ever visited. There she is living still, our Crusade mother, surrounded by her dear ones. It is fortunate for us that we have the record of the "beginnings of things" in the movement of which we are a part, penned by the faithful hand whose chirography I seem to see, "plainer than print," as I dictate these words to my stenographer here in Eastnor Castle, England, a place which I should never have beheld, in a country which would probably never have been like home to me, except for her; but which is now mapped out to the White Ribbon Movement, and led by the choicest flower of the nobility of England. And all this is because there were women who dared, women who believed in God, and went bravely forward when the Divine call had touched their hearts; and of them all, Eliza Trimble Thompson was the leader.

MAY, 20, 1895.

VI.

LETTER OF LADY HENRY SOMERSET.

205

Ionbon, August 15, 1893.

DEAR AND HONORED FRIEND:

Your charming letter has just been read to Miss
Willard and to me, and as Miss Willard is going to
send a line, I add this word of affectionate remem-
brance. You are doing a service to the cause that
will be more and more appreciated as time goes on
in giving to the great White Ribbon Army an au-
thentic record of those Origines, concerning which
you can so truly say: "All of which I saw, and part
of which I was."

We all think your Sketches should appear in
book-form, and marvel that you have so clear and
bright a pen, both figuratively and literally, after
your lifetime of care and toil.

I have been waiting in the hopes of being able
to send you one of my large photographs; but as
they are not yet finished, I send you this. The
other shall come to you as soon as possible, and
will be framed, so that, if you care to hang it up,
you will look sometimes on the face of one who
has for you the deepest sympathy and admiration.

Please remember me to Judge Thompson and
your sons and daughters, of whom Miss Willard
has often spoken.

Hoping to see you in Chicago, I am yours ever
affectionately, in White Ribbon bonds,

ISABEL SOMERSET.

www.ingramcontent.com/pod-product-compliance
Lightning Source LLC
Chambersburg PA
CBHW030115030726
47498CB00007B/2390